MW01100487

Autumn Falls

Autumn Falls

BRADFORD C. PHILEN

CHAPEL HILL
PRESS, INC.

Copyright © 2011 Bradford C. Philen

All rights reserved. No part of this book may be used, reproduced
or transmitted in any form or by any means, electronic or mechanical,
including photograph, recording, or any information storage or
retrieval system, without the express written permission
of the author, except where permitted by law.

ISBN 978-1-59715-072-9
Library of Congress Catalog Number 2010942429

First Printing

For my Mom and Dad

*We have to do with the past only as we can make it
useful to the present and the future.*

FREDERICK DOUGLASS

*I am what time, circumstance, history, have made of me, certainly,
but I am also, much more than that. So are we all.*

JAMES BALDWIN

CONTENTS

PART ONE

On a Farm in the Rural South

APPLE CIDER NIGHT

"Keith, you want a swig of this here apple cider?"

Old Dale took another gulp from the Mason jar and leaned toward his neighbor. His movements indicated the gesture was one of insistence, not of choice, for Keith.

"Well, I guess a little swallow wouldn't hurt."

It was obvious from their speech that Dale had the thicker and more down-home accent. Dale was raised and born in the holler of one of the deep green valleys lined with Galax beetleweed. Keith was an outsider, and though many thought he worked harder than any of the folk in the area, he was still, to them, just a city boy. And he did move to the area from the city, but he was no city boy. He was from the Deep South—an area more down-home, country, and filled with folk with deeper accents than anyone from the valley had ever heard.

But that was years ago. The only evidence of his hard-working upbringing were his hands. They were huge. Not skinny and lanky, but thick and powerful. Their movements were always purposeful and never lethargic. Even when he smoked a pipe, his hands seemed to grasp the wooden handle with precise control and confidence. Through years and years of hoeing the fields, picking cotton, and staking fence, his hands had acquired their gracefulness.

Keith took a hefty gulp from the jar and almost choked as the cider burned his throat. He coughed. Dale laughed.

"Don't let it hurt you now there, Keith."

"That's some potent cider. How long you let that sit for?"

With raised eyebrows, the men smiled.

"'Bout two, three days, no longer."

"Shoo-wee! You let that sit any longer I'll have to report you to the county."

"You ain't going to do that to me now, are you? What can I do to keep you hushed up?"

"You can give me two bottles."

"Shit. You want to make a profit off of my hard work."

They laughed and then settled down to a comfortable silence, passing the jar back and forth. A half an hour or more passed as the sun was just setting. The only noise was the constant chattering of the crickets and Dale's spitting into a empty golden flowerpot that sat next to his raggedy rocking chair.

"Well, I reckon it's about time for me to head on up the hill."

Keith had been anxious to leave, and in his mind he had certainly stayed long enough to be considered neighborly.

"Don't run off here, Keith."

"Keith, I got some apple pie in the oven," Nellie, Dale's robust wife, called from inside. She was knitting a cross-stitch design and watching *Wheel of Fortune* on television.

"I thank you, ma'am, but if I stay for apple pie you may not get me to leave."

"Naw, Keith, we'd kick you out before too long."

"Oh hush, Dale," Nellie chided. "Keith, don't pay no attention to him."

Keith picked up the dusty, gray Kangol off his knee and got up to leave.

"He knows I'm joshing him," Dale yelled back. "Keith, here take you another swig before you go now. It'll keep you warm in this here cold weather."

"Well...I don't want to catch cold, that's for sure."

Keith took a long sip, slowly wiped his mouth, and handed the jar back to Dale.

"Thank you much, sir."

He put on his hat and stepped to the screen door to say farewell to Nellie. "I'll be seeing you, ma'am."

"Alright, Keith. You take care now. Bring that little lady over sometime."

In Dale's old age his steps were always in hesitation. He appeared to be slow, almost feeble at times, but Dale had a wit about him that kept people on their toes.

"Yeah, buddy, I'd like to get a look at her as well."

"Oh, Dale, stop it," Nellie snapped.

Keith laughed as he stepped from the cemented porch and headed up the gravel driveway.

"Take care now, Keith."

"We'll be seeing you," Keith replied.

He passed the old dairy barn where Dale's grandfather and father had made a living. It was a two-story brick barn with tin roofing, built to outlast any of the strong winds that had been known to sweep through those cold valleys. According to Dale, it even survived a couple of tornadoes, but no one around believed him when he began telling this story; he had usually already tied one on. His tale sounded something like this:

> Shit. Y'all 'member them cold fall months back in '83, don't ya? And all-a-sudden the sky'd get all hazy and things'd feel mighty strange out. 'Fo you knew it, rains'd come out nowhere and winds'd be blowin' fierce like. Sometimes tornadoes'd be known to pick up through these here parts. On one occasion three different tornadoes came right through them forests down yonder and up the drive. One lined up behind the other. I was scared half to death—too scared to go outside and enter the basement 'cause I knew'd that if I went out, I'd be swept away. So I just held my Bible and prayed to God to ask for help 'gainst them devilish winds. I peered outta this here window

and by Golly I swear to ya them three 'nadoes couldn't fight that ol' barn. I watched all three of 'em, one at a time, try to tackle it, but that ol' barn'd just stood still. After the third one passed, the clouds went away and the sun came out. I went out to check the damages and it were bad. Trees everywhere, four dead calves lyin' 'bout, but that ol' barn ain't had not a scratch. Swear to God.

Dale's tale sounded true as he told it, but local folks would call it a fib. After that tornado storm, one could easily follow the path of the three tornadoes, each of which took a different way and altogether missed the barn by at least one hundred yards.

Keith unlatched Dale's red gate where the drive and the dirt and gravel road met. He walked up the road to his cabin atop the hill to the right of the road. The stars were shining bright, but the moon was just a sliver. Stars filled the sky. He reached the top of the hill and gazed down toward Dale's house. A small candle was lit on the porch, and the chimney exuded smoke through the navy blue sky. Nellie couldn't stand even a mildly cool house. Dale chopped firewood—not by his will or want, of course—until the late spring months of April and even May.

Keith turned toward his house and it hit him that he was half drunk. He walked down the small stone path to his porch and took the keys from his Wrangler jeans pocket.

THE DECK

Falling underneath the covers of the distant hills, the sun was on the verge of sleeping and the stars were beginning to wake. Keith sat in the brown, wooden rocker gazing at the soft, muted colors of the gentle evening sky. There was a pale blue that hovered, darkening as the Earth's atmosphere rose. Below the blue was a shade of light purple turning to magenta, then to the red, hot, sunken sun. His eyes were fixated on the stillness of the view. This was the one moment of the day that the sun could be gazed upon so obsessively without it piercing one's eyes or forcing one to bow to its magnificence.

The horizon zigzagged every which way. The area was so full of cliffs, crags, and valleys that if a giant ball was dropped from the sky it would have never ceased to ricochet.

Keith sat on the back porch that he had built himself. It had been a lengthy and almost grueling project for him. He had constantly entertained interruptions, like herding his 155 heifers from one field to another, mending two areas of fencing—one section had been destroyed by some sort of roaming forest creature, possibly running deer, but most likely a family of black bears that was known to frequent his land for wild berries. Then, there were his crops of corn, sorghum, millet, and wheat, and his garden of toma-toes, beans, peppers, potatoes, and carrots that had needed tending, and then his basement winery where he stored grape and peach wine—twenty-five-gallon buckets had to be cleaned and rotated, stoppers had to be properly tested, jugs had to be filled and stored. The porch should have been just a side doing, but, in his mind, all he had thought of was finishing it.

He'd always pictured the back deck in his mind, every angle, every two-by-four, every splinter. Once Keith planned something, he rarely thought of anything else until it was completed.

The porch stood at ten feet high. Six pillars held the platform of the deck, each one seventeen feet tall, two feet wide. They were merely wooden poles, squared in shape, but the wood was strong—oak. These poles were the columns of ancient Rome; simple in design compared to the statues and figures they held, but undoubtedly the most important architectural element. Finishing in April, it took him a total of ten months to complete.

Keith sat in one of the three rockers, gazing at the sunset, feeling the cool, brisk air of October. The day's work was exhausting—building a new hayloft in the barn that'd soon be full for the winter's supply of hay for the heifers, calves, and bulls. He was rocking; his knees were moving, but he wasn't creating the movement. The momentum of the rocker controlled his body. The oscillation of the rocker was his heartbeat. The only sound was the squeak of the rocker, the blowing of the pine needles and tree leaves, and the occasional benign mooing of a distant cow.

His thoughts wandered with fatigue. They were sporadic, uncontrolled, and sleepy. He recalled in his mind the time he was unexpectedly approached in his front lawn while constructing the middle section of the deck's floor. His visitor, a Mexican, approached him about employment. Keith was not a racist, or at least never intended to be, but his initial impressions of Mexicans were similar to the reactions of most of the people—both black and white—who lived in his area. He saw them as a burden, one looking for a handout, rather than a man looking for an opportunity. Keith saw the Mexican as unclean and greasy, a man only suited for simple labor, like digging holes and janitorial duties, cursed never to wear business attire.

The Mexican American population had steadily increased in a neighboring county, and he'd read the articles about the crime and drug rates of the slums where they lived and figured Mexicans only wanted farm work to secretly grow marijuana. He'd heard their women were prostitutes and carried diseases. Keith had even heard that these people were all cousins to one another and accepted interfamily marriages. These weren't his opinions; he chose to accept these myths about the "spics" because it was easy to believe them and he had no reason to see it differently.

Dale often used derogatory terms to refer to minorities and never hesitated to stand by a story he'd just heard as if it were a Bible tale. Though Keith never went so far, he laughed at the jokes like the locals and shook his head with disgust when hearing the arrest stories. He even tried to stare down these people in public. Keith was afraid of these people that he denied to understand or to listen to. He wasn't racist in nature, but a victim of ignorance.

On that day it had been approximately eleven o'clock. The Mexican's car had descended down the road from the north. Keith looked up the hill as the car descended. He didn't gaze long, only enough time to recognize it was an unfamiliar car and then dropped his head back to the wood pieces that lay before him.

The car continued and finally parked by a narrow pull-off just past Keith's mailbox. Half of his car was still in the middle of the dirt road, but on that road two cars seldom passed one another, so it didn't matter.

It was an old vehicle. Not by years, but it had aged and become worn through the hundreds of thousands of miles it had traveled. As the mystery man turned off the ignition, the '86 tan Honda stalled and jumped forward. The doors had noticeable dents, each one telling a new fender-bender story or parking lot bruising. The passenger side back door had layers of black plastic trash bags taped to the frame of the window. The tires had mismatched hubcaps; one was a small spare, too small to fit the car properly. The front windshield had two cracks, the front left headlight was busted, and the vehicle was missing the passenger side-view mirror. The man sat for a moment, stalled, like his car. He didn't notice Keith's stare.

The stranger's presence was puzzling to Keith. He knew that Tommy Cox, who lived down by Kelly's Cove in the valleys of a neighboring mountain area, had hired Mexicans to bail his hay, but only because his wife was sick in the hospital and he hadn't been able to be there for the work. Other than that Keith had never heard of any Mexicans living or working in the immediate area. He was anxious to find out what the spic wanted.

The indention at the car door joint forced a deep waning sound as the man exited his vehicle. Approaching Keith, the man watched the ground, taking each stride slowly and cautiously; there were tools and wood pieces scattered on the grass. He cleared the knot in his throat and spoke.

"Good afternoon, sir."

Keith stared in the Mexican's eyes and then looked down at the extended tape measure in his hands. His movements were protracted, subdued, and quiet.

Snap.

"Hello," Keith said in a voice that mimicked his movements.

They stood motionless for what seemed like minutes. Keith noticed the worn clothes of the man. His brown boots were dusty and unpolished, the right heel was slightly split, his faded blue jeans were decorated with what looked like white paint splotches, his faded purple and dark blue plaid shirt was tucked into his jeans, and he wore a faded blue baseball hat, slightly tilted, that read "Fosters." He wasn't a tall man. His jet-black sideburns were thick and cut just below the top of his ears. The smoothness of his forehead, his black and bushy eyebrows, and his jet-black eyes showed in the midday sun. His eyes were tired, but alert. Red lines ran from the irises to the inner part of his eye socket, like a river runs into a delta. His facial skin was smooth and almost ageless, like a child's. The width of his nose accentuated his wide and chubby cheekbones. His mustache was perfectly trimmed. He didn't fit the description of the Mexican men Keith had encountered in town. Most wore tight, dark blue jeans, cowboy boots, brightly colored cotton button-down shirts, and ten-gallon hats.

In reality, the pause did not last long, only seconds.

"What can I do you for?"

"I come to ask to work."

His Tex-Mex accent was thick and his speech was hesitant. Keith wanted to find out more about this man, as if that would tell him who they all were.

"Where do you live?"

The man raised his eyebrows.

"My house?"

"Hmm-mmm."

"I live at Independence by the courthouse."

"By the courthouse?"

"Yes, sir."

"Where are you from?"

"Mexico."

Keith's knowledge of Mexico was slight. He could only think of two cities, the capital and a tourist party city where his son had visited during a school holiday.

"Where in Mexico?"

"Queretaro."

"Come again."

His pronunciation sounded like one long continuous rolled "r." The man repeated more slowly, but Keith still didn't quite hear what he said.

There was a pause.

Keith looked again at the tape measure in his hand and then to the man.

"Well, what kind of work are you looking for?"

"My cousin hear you make wine from grapes and peaches. I can trim bushels and thorns … pick peaches."

Grapevines were very fragile and difficult to maintain. If they were trimmed too short or left unattended for too long, the grapes would be unmanageable. Keith was curious as to where he'd learned about winery production. Most of the major wineries in the region would not hire immigrants, so far as he knew.

"Have you worked at Asheville?"

"Ashe…ville? No, I was live in Sonoma, California. I did work for Belmont."

Belmont wines were popular, though Keith disliked them. Sonoma was the wining capital of America, an area full of grape fields and cheap labor. Keith had never been to California.

"California? Hmm-mmm. You know, I don't have too many grape bushels. It's really just enough for me to work."

"Oh. Okay. My cousin not know and I think I will ask."

Their conversation was over, but Keith had many questions and thoughts circling his mind. He wasn't sure how to ask them, but he wanted to know how he got here from California, and how he got to California from Mexico. He wanted to know whom his cousin worked for and how he would have known he was making wine. He wondered how many cousins he had. He wanted to smell his home, his food.

The Mexican turned away and walked to his car. The door made the same deep, waning sound. Keith stared as if he could find the answers to his questions if only he looked hard enough. He noticed the backseat held a hard black case made for some kind of horn instrument. He wondered what instrument was inside and what music he played. His searching for answers only led to more questions. The man sat inside the vehicle and shut the door. The car miss-started once and then revved. He drove down the hill, continuing south, never once looking back to Keith.

After the vehicle was well down the road, Keith placed the tape measure on the workbench and went inside. He walked through his clustered living room and into his workroom that had a large desk with papers stacked in numerous piles, a couple of file cabinets, and two tall bookshelves. Most of the books were hard-covered history volumes about the American Revolutionary War and the Civil War. He scanned through an old set of encyclopedias he had bought at a yard sale for thirteen dollars. Cobwebs covered the crevices of the old bookshelf. He reached for "M." It made the ruffling and cracking sound of a new book.

Keith found the section of Mexican maps. After some time he found the name Queretaro. It was a boldfaced title, a state of Mexico. It was a large state compared to the others and lay in the central area of the country. Keith gazed for a moment at all the different names and areas, which were, to him, nothing more. He wondered where in Queretaro the Mexican was from and what his life was like before he came to the States.

Keith regretted not engaging in further dialogue. That was his life, it seemed: full of spurts of joyful and sullen moments and that ever present feeling of regret for all that he did—regret not only for the bad but the good as well. He shut the book and returned it to its proper place. He walked back through his living room and to the deck work outside.

∽

Keith often thought of that day and of his own distant past. Memories came in bits and pieces, here and there. He was hesitantly attached to his memories; contrite first and then responsible, but the farm always took precedence. The bails of hay would be brought next week by Johnny Russell and his son, who lived across the county line to the north just past Independence, the same Independence where the Mexican lived. The late-blooming tomatoes had to be picked from the garden. Tomatoes were his weakness. He could never walk past juicy tomatoes without picking or buying a few. Growing up on tomato and mayonnaise sandwiches was the catalyst for this addiction.

Keith looked down the sloping hill. The pine trees were growing and had survived the last three early frosts of fall. He knew they would live longer than he and eventually grow high above his home. Someday he'd have to cut them so he could gaze out at the vista that was before him now.

It was almost dark. He could scarcely see Crackel Mountain to his right. The hill was large and smooth. Trees covered the sides of the slopes of the hill, but the top was bare, less the grass and alfalfa. Dale had told Keith that would be the best spot to build a home. Keith had agreed it would be a great site for a view, but he knew it would be too cold from the blowing winds.

The mountain looked frigid. The trees on the sides fiercely swayed because of the valley wind. The night was due to have a new moon, so the sky would be full of stars. Mars was already shining brightly, opposite Keith and the sinking sun.

With the darkness came the sounds of night. The neighbor's dogs began barking at the mysterious darkness. They always barked during the new and full moon phases. The locusts began chirping. Though none of the sounds seemed to be related, they exuded a serene harmony. Keith continued rocking, occasionally falling in and out of consciousness.

Through the Motions

Early the next morning Keith began with the firewood. Freshly cut pieces were scattered to his left and right. He bought the logs from Old Dale at a reasonably cheap price—a truckload for seventy-five dollars. Keith had plenty of wood; he had three different piles underneath his back deck.

From the cold air Keith could see his breath. He wore his brown work boots, two pairs of wool socks, a pair of old work jeans, a white undershirt, a long-sleeved cotton shirt, a red and black flannel button-down, and a black beanie.

As a base for the splitting he used the trunk of a large pine that he had cut so he could build his back deck. The trunk was massive. The rings were dark, like shoe polish. He regretted cutting it; it was a part of the hill, just as the old and weathered house was. After it was down, the slope looked lonely.

He could feel the muscles in his back working. He was sore, but it was a pleasant feeling: one produced by hard work, nothing too strenuous, just the right amount of exerted force. He stopped to place another log on the pine and spotted the heifers and calves on the top of Crackel Mountain. They were taking in the warmth of the sun, slowly making their way down the hill to the pasture of short grass.

Keith typically rotated the cows every two days. He had a total of 155 calves, which he would sell to the highest-paying buyer the following March. From there the calves would take a road trip either to Kansas or

California—to some corporation-controlling feedlot—for further grazing and growth. Then they would be sold, slaughtered, and sent to the corporate meat markets. Keith didn't make a lot of money from the calves, only about five hundred dollars a head, depending on their exact weight. He had two hundred acres to graze the young cows and send them on the assembly-lined meat market.

There was more money to be made in the cow business, but Keith stayed away from it. After he sold his cattle they would surely be injected with steroids. Keith, as well as many other cow farmers, disagreed with this tactic. Even the cow farmers that did give injections often disagreed, but ethics was no longer an issue. The market mattered the most. If a cow farmer couldn't produce enough weight in his cattle, then the cattle wouldn't sell well. Keith had met several cow farmers in the area who hadn't produced a profit over the last several years because of this competition. Corporations were in charge of the market, as they had been since the American railroad expansion of the early 1900s.

He set the last log on the pine trunk and swung, striking directly in the middle.

THUMP.

The axe fell three-fourths of the way down the log. Keith used more force than usual. He unwedged the axe and swung one more time.

THUMP.

CRACK.

The piece was split. He walked to the side of the house and leaned the axe against the wall.

Keith gathered a small number of pieces at a time to carry and to stack. Each returning trip he tried to place one more log so to finish more quickly. His body wasn't in a hurry, but his mind was; he knew he had more work ahead of him.

It took him roughly an hour to finish stacking, to clean the area of wood chips and debris, and to return the equipment to the work shed beyond the fence of the backyard. The shed was a small structure, simple in construction, built to hold yard and garden tools and equipment. He kept his larger farming equipment and machinery in the red barn down the hill.

He returned from the shed and entered the basement door under the deck. The basement was large. It had a cold and gray cement floor. Directly opposite the door there was a washing machine and dryer he used during the fall and winter months. During spring and summer he usually washed his clothes by hand to save water from his ever-dwindling well. He wasn't sure how much time would pass before the well actually went dry—he figured another five or six years—but he always did what he could to prolong a new digging.

Next to the washer and dryer there were shelves full of Mason jars of preserves. Apple butter, tomatoes, green beans, beets, corn, and other vegetables and berries lined the shelves. The staircase, which led to the upstairs part of the house, divided the middle of the basement floor. One side, the side closest to the washer and dryer, was cluttered with boxes of old tools, various types of nails, screws, bolts, washers—all organized by size—pipes, tin cans full of random materials, and stacks of two-by-four pieces of plywood. Though it was cluttered to the naked eye and seemed to be a camouflaged area of who knew what, he knew exactly where everything was and could get to what he wanted.

On the other side of the basement staircase were ten different twenty-five-gallon plastic trash bins. Each bin had a large glass cylinder, which held fermenting and aging wine. He had six cylinders of grape wine and four of peach. Each container was plugged by a transparent stopper and held a temperature gauge. Too high a temperature would turn the sorghum and sugar mixture to vinegar and spoil the taste of the wine. Too much sorghum and sugar content and the wine would yield too much alcohol. It was Keith's chemistry project and he had learned to be the professor, a wine artist. He knew the right mixtures to produce a sweet wine, a dry wine, a strong wine, and a wine that didn't produce an unwanted aftertaste.

Keith had an acre and a half of the Grape Woody vines that produce the Vinefera red and white grapes, and he had an acre of peach trees. Early fall was the best time to pick, when they have just ripened. Before crushing the fruit, he picked off some of the grape skins, but not all, because the skins added color and some of the taste to the wine. He then filled the glass containers three-fourths full, after which he added yeast and sorghum, and then filled the remaining container with more fruit juices. He added the stoppers, which held the temperature gauges. The gauges were so sensitive that Keith had to clean and rotate them every two days. If the temperature of the fermenting wine reached above eighty degrees Fahrenheit, he added ice to the plastic bins. If the temperature dropped below sixty-eight degrees Fahrenheit, he would remove the ice or pour warm water in the bins.

The fermentation process took about two weeks. If he wanted a sweeter wine he added sherry to the fruits immediately after crushing the grapes. This quickened the fermentation process and yielded less alcohol. For a dry wine he added sherry after fermentation was complete and allowed the bottled wine to sit for a month or more.

This was the fourth year that he had made his homemade concoction. He sold most of the wines at ten or fifteen dollars a bottle. He had received numerous compliments, and several customers had asked him to put the wine on the market.

∽

After examining the temperature gauges Keith headed to his old, beat-up Ford F-100 pickup to check on the cattle on Crackel Mountain.

It was a '74 Ford, four-wheel drive, twelve-cylinder. The many dents and bruises seemed to hold the vehicle intact. It was light yellow, almost off-white. Thirty-two-inch tires suspended the truck. Keith had the bed of the truck removed and hired Dale to lay a steel frame bed instead. He could fit 20 bales if they were stacked properly. The inside cab was just as beat up as the outside. Dust sat thick on the dashboard, on the glass piece that shielded the various meters, on the vents that barely worked, on the glove compartment that had a huge hole underneath it, and on the torn black leather seats. The passenger-side seat was split, and foam stuck out from it; the driver seat was lined with duct tape. The inside panel of the passenger side door was missing, making for an even colder drive. The floorboards were as soiled as the earth. The stick shift was a long pole that sprouted from the floorboard. The handle had long been missing, and a nut-and-bolt-rigged handle was in its place.

Keith slowly drove down the hill and noticed the leaves were beginning to change. Hovering high above Crackel Mountain he spotted six vultures soaring in a perfect circle. They were graceful, death-searching creatures.

Keith reached the gates to his fields and went through the process of opening the gates, driving through, and then closing the gates. He thought of all the times he had done the same thing over and over. He could have done it in his sleep. Farm life seemed monotonous and slow to many, but what life wasn't, Keith wondered. To Keith there was a new job every moment. There was always the same task of mending fence, but always in a different place.

Keith was in the largest fenced field, about forty-five acres. It was covered with short grass and two large areas of forest; one sloped down each side of Crackel Mountain. Down the right-side slope most of the trees were evergreen—spruce and pine—while descending the left side most were hardwood oaks and maples. Crackel Mountain showed the diversity of the area. During the spring months wildflowers bloomed, and Keith could spot every color of the rainbow.

Crackel Mountain had been so named because of the exuding crackling sounds of tree limbs on windy days. It was called a mountain, but it was more of a hill, elevated at about twenty-five hundred feet. Dale had told him it was called a mountain simply because it was the highest spot in the area. Upon the heath Keith had also planted alfalfa, which grew quickly and gave the cattle nutrients and minerals in multitudes that the grass couldn't provide. The only downside to growing alfalfa was that deer loved it as well. Deer were a nuisance; they ate the nutritious grass planted specifically for the cows. Sometimes Keith took his truck spotlighting just to count the deer. There were numerous nights he sat in awe and couldn't count them all. Keith never allowed hunting on his land, though it was certainly a haven for hunters. *No trespassing, no firearm* signs were posted throughout his territory. Every November he was bombarded by hunters, usually father-and-son duos, who would ask to shoot on his land. Keith wasn't against hunting, but he didn't trust the hunters. The last thing he wanted was to have to trust someone with his property. What if a gate was left open and cattle got loose? What about the fences that would be damaged in the chase? Worse even, what if someone was shot on his land? He had heard of these incidents before and figured they could just as easily happen on his land. It boiled down to he knew how he wanted things done, *no if, ands, or buts.*

Keith spotted the cattle where he thought they would be—scattered on the right side of the hill so that the mid-morning sun warmed them. Some roamed by the edge of the tree line, some sat in the sun, and some just chomped the grass.

Cows were intelligent, but certainly not adventurous animals. They were easy to tend. They could always be found in the vicinity of one another. Keith's cattle were trained. They had rotated fields on the same schedule since April. They knew exactly which field led to the next, and had even managed to measure the days accordingly. Often Keith found his cattle waiting by the gate to be moved, as if to say, "You're late, where you been?"

Keith continued up the hill and parked atop of Crackel Mountain. The grass on the lot was still thick, thick like his granddaddy's blond hair. His granddaddy had always bragged about his hair; holding his small black comb with the narrow teeth, he would tell Keith, "One thing's for sure, you're a Baker and you'll never be bald."

Keith walked down the right side of Crackel Mountain and approached the cattle. He walked hesitantly and slowly and spoke with a soft and repetitious tone, "Sue-cow, sue-cow, sue-cow." He reached out his arm as if to pet them. His pace was always slow and cautious—smooth with the pace of his rural world. The cattle would stare at him with the look of blind eyes and instinctively gnaw on the green grass. They weren't scared of Keith, but any sort of human activity startled them. Constant sounds of excreted feces and urine spilled into the coolness and quietude of the day.

"Sue-cow, sue-cow, sue-cow."

With herding cows the tactic was to get at least a handful going in the right direction; the rest would follow. Keith convinced a few, and the heifers knew exactly which way to go. Their hooves heavily stomped the fertile green land. There were twenty or so scattered about feeding on grass and another huddled group that noticed the herd and little by little followed as well.

Keith made a head count, but only reached seventy-seven. He recounted, but got the same number. He took his time scanning the forests, glancing through the thick pines, but didn't see the one missing mammal. Since all but one were accounted for, he decided to move the cattle in the new field and then to continue his search for the lone cow gone astray.

A stray cow wasn't unusual. Keith thought nothing of it. Walking to the gate he grabbed a piece of thick grass to gnaw. Instinctive and unconscious actions and movements were common on the farm. Emotion was rarely necessary, as was true with Keith as well. Life simply existed as a partnership with the Earth.

The cattle made a path. Keith climbed the fence by the joint side, then crossed the dirt and gravel road to unlock the fence to the next field. He pushed the gate open. He walked back and unlatched the occupied field fence, cautiously pushing the fence so as not to scare the herd. They sidestepped and wavered—then, out of anxiety, sprinted to the new field full of high grass. Hurriedly they entered and then dispersed, enticed by the thicker and greener pasture. The sun shone bright and the temperature was rising. He counted one more time and again there were only seventy-seven.

Keith adjusted his hat so it sat high on his head, and he again noticed the swarming vultures. This time there were nine; three more had joined the brigade. Keith spotted the orange heads of three turkey vultures. The others were black vultures. He could name all the types of vultures just as he could identify most of the plants and animals in the area. Vultures had huge claws and rounded beaks. They were dark in color and flocked in groups.

∽

On one day during the winter Keith spotted over a hundred in the sky. They were so thick where they flew, the sky looked like gray smoke. A horse had died at the Smith's farm. Paul and Nancy had gone to visit Nancy's mother in town. It had snowed and sleeted all that night. Paul and Nancy weren't able to get back. All the roads were too slick; it was an unexpected winter storm. Telephone lines and trees were down, and two-inch-thick ice lined the roads. They were stuck for three days. On the second day Keith drove the truck down to his barn and spotted the scavengers. He continued to investigate and tally the damages of the area. When he got to the spot where the vultures hovered, he saw their horse General dead on the ground. There were twenty or more of the carrion hunters clawing and scratching at the horse's strong calves and broad shoulders. He had been little more than a skeleton when Keith had finally arrived. General had gotten spooked during the night of the first sleet and managed to get out of the fenced barn area. Through the night General couldn't survive the cold and died. The next day, the vultures swarmed.

∽

The nine new vultures brought this memory back to Keith. He crossed the road again and walked up the hill to his truck. He figured he could make more ground in the truck, and if the cow was dead he could get to it before the vultures did too much picking.

Keith drove along a small path to the left of Crackel Mountain. The path was just wide enough for his truck to maneuver. A thick forest of hardwood trees lined both sides of the path. Years and years of brown leaves had packed the ground.

As the road opened to a small meadow Keith spotted three vultures and the missing cow. The vultures had just landed and were approaching the wounded animal. They were ten or more feet from the heifer. Keith stepped on the gas and wildly blew the horn. The vultures scattered away and flew back to their flock. Keith parked close to the cow. Before stepping out of the vehicle, he threw his hat against the front windshield.

The cow was lying on her right side. Her tail was flapping at the flies on its side. She was still alive. Her right hoof was twitching, as a dog's paw would while in a deep dream. Her mouth was open and her dark tongue lay hanging, slobbering on the grass. Her right eye was shut, nestled by the ground. Her left eye was open, but unconscious to Keith and the flesh-eating scavengers. Dried tears ran from her eye and her nostrils. She breathed deeply and made soft but deep sounds of pain.

It was a shotgun wound. Keith could see the deep hole, clogged with tissue, cartilage, and ligament. The surrounding areas of her body were wet with sweat. Keith envisioned what had happened. Just beyond the meadow were briers of berries. The cow was walking through the meadow during the early morning and was shot by a hunter mistaking the brute for a deer. Keith was sure there were old deer stands in the nearby forests. While he prohibited hunting, his land was too large to constantly monitor.

The story fit, but Keith didn't understand how the cow was still alive. He figured she was shot at least six hours earlier. The brute was in mortal pain, and Keith had to find a way to put it out of its misery and dispose of the carcass so the vultures wouldn't get it. He didn't have a gun in his truck, and if he left the animal, the vultures would certainly eat her alive.

Keith scanned the area and spotted a large stone, shaped like an anvil, where the path continued past the meadow. He walked to the rock and figured it weighed thirty-five or forty pounds. He carried it to the cow and set it down by her front hooves. The cow was still moaning. Her left eye stared ahead, showing only a glimpse of life. Keith took a deep breath. The vultures were circling. Their number was growing, and the sky was eerily softening.

In one swift movement Keith lifted the stone above his head and thrust the rock of the Earth, shaped like an anvil, on the breathing animal's head.

THUMP.

The cow howled. The cow moaned. Keith reached for the heavy stone once again.

THUMP.

CRACK.

The cow's skull split and the Earth was still again. With the second strike of the stone her body twitched once more and then her legs no longer ran in her deadening-dream state of mind. The vultures still swarmed. Keith could feel the muscles in his back, the same muscles he used earlier in the morning to chop the firewood. He was exhausted physically and mentally. Keith hunched over the animal, breathing fast, having exerted too much force.

After resting momentarily Keith hauled fallen and dead tree limbs to the fresh carcass and made a bonfire. The exuding smoke from the burning animal carcass diverted the vultures, and the blue sky opened once again.

Flour and Flowers

Weeks had passed since the death of the cow. Being insured was important with cow farming. Keith was often overcautious and had more than enough insurance to be recompensated. The hunter was never found, but Keith thought he knew who the culprits were. He searched the thick woods near the meadow and found two deer stands, one covered with plastic Pepsi bottles, an empty pack of Red Man, and a tin of Skoal Mint. It was a juvenile. Keith knew an adult wouldn't leave such evidence.

He figured it was Jack and Charlie Barr, Tommy Cox's nephews. They lived some six or seven miles away and attended Independence High School. Whenever Keith ran into him, Tommy mentioned the boys and their interest in hunting. Keith told Tommy his land wasn't open to hunting, but Tommy made it sound like a family matter, saying, "Those boys'll treat your land just like they was your sons." Tommy had an easygoing, everyone-is-family attitude, and assumed everyone felt the same. Keith obviously didn't. He didn't want Tommy's family hospitality.

Keith didn't have enough proof that the boys did it, but he called Tommy to tell him about what had happened.

"Well, Keith, I'm sorry to hear that."

"Well, Tommy, just make sure your nephews know they are not allowed to hunt my land."

"Keith, you don't think that."

"No, I don't know. But I want you to tell them to stay off my land."

Tommy was taken aback by what Keith said, but Keith knew Tommy wouldn't get upset enough to raise his voice over the issue; he was too easygoing.

In those weeks that passed Keith spent most of his evenings and nights with Whitney. They'd known each other for three or four years, but had only been intimate for just over a year. Not too many people knew about their relationship. Whitney had once read in some novel that a secret and quiet love was like a peaceful sleep.

∽

Keith slowly opened his eyes to her red cotton summer shirt and the white sweater that lay crumpled and thrown on the hardwood floor from last night's undressing. He could hear the running faucet in the kitchen and the bubbling sound of brewing coffee, though the steamed grounds had not yet aromatized the air.

Looking at the floor, Keith noticed Whitney's clothing randomly thrown about. One would have thought it was a night of sweat and racing heartbeats, but it was only a night of tight holds and gentle touches. She often undressed and threw her clothes on the ground, not thinking twice about them. This aroused Keith, but he never revealed it to her. He refrained from words of adoration, even praise, because he didn't quite know how to do either. To the unfamiliar eye he was austere, even stark. He dreaded receiving praise and even simple gestures of thanks, and as a result Keith avoided giving them as well. They made him uncomfortable. He disliked the never-ending cycle of the thank-you. There was complete falseness, even buffoonery in it, Keith thought. He had witnessed too many special favors and pats-on-the-backs within bureaucratic city ceremonies and government meetings. As the son of a sharecropping family, he had been raised to cherish with caution and a quiet mouth your blessings and good tidings. In his present life, his rural life, individuals on the outside were narcissistic at best, Keith thought. He was harsh, but with innocent intention.

Keith rolled over in bed. His head fell to the pillow and her scent shot through the thin cotton pillowcase. It wasn't remarkably strong, but it was *her*: alluring to Keith, even tasty, like a sweet peach on a sweltering summer day. He closed his eyes again and could smell the brewing coffee, slowly trickling through the hallway and into the bedroom. The morning sun began to light the room. Roosters cried. Even though it was October, Whitney always opened the window. She liked the air to be cool and the covers to be warm and plentiful.

Keith opened his eyes again. His bare legs could feel the contrast in temperature. Keith's bones and joints cracked, like the hardwood floors. Constant work had made his body sore to wake.

Keith staggered to the kitchen and stared at Whitney washing dishes. Her back was bare. Her dark brown hair lay just past her neck. Her shoulders were smooth, yet faintly defined. Keith noticed the roundness of her breasts. *So soft*, Keith thought. She wore only her red satin and silk panties. Keith noticed the design of the waistband and the small blue bruise just below her firm butt.

Whitney often sang in the kitchen.

"Close your eyes and think of me … mmm … mmmm … mmmm … mmmm…."

Keith slyly stepped closer and closer until he was behind her. With the backs of his hands he gently stroked her soft skin where her buttocks and thighs met. She paused, then continued washing.

"I thought I heard you."

Keith was quiet. He stepped even closer, slowly parted her chocolate hair with the tips that curled, and delicately blew on the back of her neck. He moved his hands, stroking the outside of her thighs. She lowered her head so that he could get to every spot. She turned and their eyes met. They kissed. Their lips hadn't yet parted, but Keith uttered.

"What's for breakfast?"

Whitney moved her head away from his.

"Ha. It's your house. You tell me."

Their arms were wrapped about each other.

"Well. I'll tell you, but you're cooking."

"Fine. You can't cook anyways."

"Hey, now."

With his left hand Keith reached to the cabinet on his left.

"You drinking coffee?"

"Yeah. You?"

"Yes, ma'am."

Whitney loved it when he said, "Yes, ma'am" to her. She folded her arms and rested them on her tummy, giving Keith a full frontal of her breasts. They sat perked, plump, and rotund. Her nipples were hard from the coolness of the air. With reluctance, Keith found Whitney's eyes.

"Milk … right, no sugar?"

"Yes, sir."

"Coming right up."

He stepped to the fridge to get the milk.

"So what am I cooking?" Whitney prodded.

She grinned and Keith sighed playfully. His speech was slow.

"Oh, I don't know. How about pancakes?"

"Buttermilk?"

"There ain't no other kind."

"I guess I can handle that."

"I'll turn on the radio and then I reckon I'll sit, sip on this here coffee, read yesterday's paper, and, uh, as they say, watch the view."

She laughed and looked to her breasts, which she was very proud of.

"I can shut the blinds if I'm too undone for your neighbors."

"No, no. Then, uh, there wouldn't be no view. Who needs neighbors anyway?"

Their eyes met again. She was smiling wide and he was grinning, like a boy who'd gotten away with a prank.

They listened to the *Saturday Morning Bluegrass Session* from the local radio station WBRF 98.7. Whitney's first cousin Jerry was the host of the two-hour-long show, which played only demos and albums of local bands. The show was popular throughout the region. Even folks in Winston-Salem tried listening in and had made requests for the show to be broadcast on a corporate channel. Jerry refused though, saying corporate channels were more concerned with making money than playing music. This was the story he told the city channel delegates and executives at least. To the locals, he had a more xenophobic or nationalistic notion. He told them he would do whatever he could to keep mountain music in the mountains. Through some two hundred years or more, bonds had been made and communities built because of the music, and Jerry did not want to be the one to take the music away from those communities. Jerry *believed* in the history of the area, and if the music somehow changed, the way of life would change as well. Bluegrass music was the indisputable foundation of the souls of the people, and the Blue Ridge Mountains were the sturdy frame of their core.

Jerry had the ideal radio voice: neither too deep, nor too high. He pronounced words fittingly, though not always correctly, and at the right pace. A touch of the local accent rattled the microphone. He was never too excited. The energy in his voice was constant but calm, and he was a walking history book of bluegrass music. Much of the music had been passed-down folktales, and Jerry had a story, an anecdote, and a character for every song he played on the radio.

As they listened, the music turned up loud so that it filled the house, Keith and Whitney were occupied. In between glances to Whitney's bare torso, he read the *Gazette*, a biweekly newspaper from Esmont, the closest town. It was a minor paper. Keith read every article, though he often laughed to himself about the local news and headlines. Usually on Saturday the front-page headlines told who won the previous night's high school game. Then there would be articles about the locals' concern for a new streetlight, a new Walmart opening in the next county, and a choir group's singing schedules. Keith always spotted grammar errors, and often the pictures had no captions or order; they randomly drifted through the pages.

He appreciated and valued, however, the *Gazette* for the same reasons he laughed at it. This was the news, his life before him, and he didn't feel the need to know news outside of it. There was no news in D.C., Nashville, or even Richmond that could have affected his security. He was far removed from those places and those worlds.

Whitney was busy making the pancakes. She prepared the batter on the small island that sat in the middle of the kitchen. The ingredients and utensils before her were a large bowl, a small bowl, a couple of tablespoons, a fork, two bananas, a carton of buttermilk, a carton of milk, eggs, butter, baking powder, flour, cinnamon, vanilla, and two Mason jars filled with sugar and salt.

With one egg in each hand, she cracked them on the edge of a stainless steel bowl, a trick she had mastered by watching her grandmother in the kitchen. The yolks oozed and then drooled from their shells. She added a quarter cup of milk and beat the mixture. In the large bowl she squashed the bananas and then doused them with a cup of buttermilk. She felt the mushiness of the bananas and the lumpiness of the buttermilk slide between her fingers. She added baking powder, salt, and sugar. Her measurements were more estimated than exact, however always yielded scrumptious cuisine.

She beat the combined bowls and then added a touch of cinnamon. With the skillet she melted three tablespoons of butter. While the butter sat bubbling and simmering, she added flour—a cup at a time—to the batter and stirred. She stirred fast, but smoothly, not spilling any of the flour. The batter thickened. She poured the melted butter from the skillet into the larger bowl and finally added a touch of vanilla.

The pancakes took little time to cook on the skillet. The room smelled of the buttermilk batter and the cooking cakes, overpowering the scent of the brewed coffee grounds. The morning slowly passed, and the sun lit the house through the surrounding windows. Keith casually looked to Whitney and spotted a spill of batter on her breast.

The phone rang but was faintly heard over the screaming fiddle blasting from the radio. Whitney and Keith looked to each other. Keith finished his sip of coffee and caught the phone on the sixth ring. He had no answering machine and generally disliked the phone and conversations through wires.

"Hello."

Whitney continued cooking.

There was a pause.

"Well, yes, ma'am, it is. Who might this be?"

There was a pause.

"Daffney Smith?"

Keith's surprised voice heightened.

"From Pineapple? Well, I declare. How are you doing?"

There was a pause.

"Mmm…mmm."

There was a pause.

"Mmm…mmm…No, ma'am, I haven't heard from him in some time."

Keith's tone began to change. His body leaned against the kitchen door frame and his eyes scanned the room, occasionally finding Whitney.

There was a pause.

"Mmm…mmm."

His tone floated deeper and deeper. Whitney hesitated and looked to Keith. Keith's body language gradually shifted, slouched, sagged. He turned away from the kitchen.

There was a pause.

"How did it happen?"

Whitney stopped. She picked up her coffee and leaned against the sink counter, watching Keith's broad and muscular back.

"Mmm…mmm."

There was a pause.

She admired the broadness of his shoulders and even the love handles that were beginning to form around his side.

There was a pause.

"When's the funeral?"

Whitney's face hardened. "Funeral," she repeated and sighed. She set down her coffee mug and covered her bare breasts with her forearms, as if to shield her from the worst.

"Next Sunday?"

There was a pause.

Whitney looked to the skillet. It had begun to smoke. She turned down the burner and plopped another scoop of butter on the skillet. The butter sizzled and melted. The smoke subsided.

"Mmm ... mmm."

There was a pause.

The room had become cold. Keith turned toward the kitchen and saw the last of the butter melt. The tone of the morning transformed. Whitney poured a cup of batter on the oily skillet.

"Mmm ... mmm."

There was a pause.

"Okay."

There was a pause.

Keith watched Whitney walk to bedroom. She dressed.

"Mmm ... mmm."

There was a pause.

"Well, thank you for calling, Daffney. How's your family?"

There was a pause.

"Mmm ... mmm. Tell your mother and Tommy I said hello."

There was a pause.

Whitney returned to the kitchen and leaned against the counter, once again watching Keith.

"Okay. Mmm ... mmm. I'll see you. Okay ... Bye-bye."

Keith hung up the phone and turned to Whitney. He anxiously scanned the kitchen. A stack of pancakes sat on the white plate with the faded wildflower design. Whitney leaned against the counter; her arms crossed at her waist. She, too, was anxious. She wanted to go to him, but knew he would distance himself.

There was a pause.

"You okay?" Whitney finally asked.

He looked down to the white linoleum floor and then to Whitney wearing the white sweater she had pulled off the night before.

"Yeah, I'm okay."

"What happened?"

"That was a friend from back home. She said that Billy died."

There was a pause.

"Apparently he had just gotten out of the county jail and went home, carrying a twelve-pack of beer. After that no one heard from him for two or so days, so a neighbor went to see if he was alright. No one answered the door when he knocked, so that afternoon a couple of the neighbors busted down the back door. They found him dead sitting at the kitchen table."

Whitney sighed. As if sick to her stomach, she covered her mouth. The white fluorescent light in the kitchen flickered.

"Oh my. What happened?"

"They guessed he was half-drunk. He drank maybe ten or eleven of the beers and went to smoke a cigarette. He lit the cigarette with the gas stove and blew out the flame. But he forgot to turn off the gas. He probably passed out shortly after from the alcohol and through the night died of carbon monoxide poisoning."

"Lawd, lawd," Whitney said in her thick local accent, which she could turn on and off like a switch. She was astonished. Keith smirked. *What a dumb ass*, he thought. She continued.

"When'd you talk to him last?"

Keith looked up to the white ceiling paint as if it was a crystal ball that could reveal to him his last meeting, the last conversation with his brother.

There was a pause.

"I guess it's been over two years. He called me one night drunk at some type of party or concert. I couldn't really hear his voice."

"Mmm ... a late-night drunk call."

Keith looked to Whitney's eyes.

"Yeah, he was saying something like, 'I'm sorry,' or, 'Can we be friends,' but I couldn't make it out. I think I hung up on him."

Keith's eyes now pierced Whitney. *Had he become distant*, she wondered. She looked down. She noticed a small hole at the left forearm of her white sweater. Keith continued to look to her.

"The funeral is next week. I was thinking. Mmm ... You wanna go?"

There was a pause.

Surprised, Whitney looked up again and met his eyes. *Was this what he really wanted?* she thought. The white fluorescent light flickered again.

"I'll have to replace that," Keith said.

There was a pause.

"So?" Keith questioned.

"Sure," she said.

"Can Mike stay with Michael?"

Whitney had momentarily forgotten her eleven-year-old son.

"Oh ... yeah, I'm sure it'll be alright. I'll call his daddy today."

"Alright. I reckon I'll get a couple of plane tickets. Maybe we can rent a car down there."

There was a pause.

"Alright ... Keith, you alright?"

There was a pause.

Their eyes met again. Neither smiled. Keith was still anxious. Whitney sealed the bag of white flour sitting on the island.

"We got pancakes," she said.

"Buttermilk?"

"There ain't no other kind," Whitney said and grinned.

PART TWO

A Trip Home

Sweet Home Alabama

"That's where my grandpa worked every Sunday or so. He wasn't much of a churchgoer."

They drove slowly through the lone, lightless street named Main Street.

"What kind of shop was it?" Whitney asked, staring at the abandoned two-story red-brick building.

"Well, the way my ma told it, it was first an old post office, one of the first in this area. But since no one seemed to get mail, the owner changed it into a small hardware store. But then folks were too poor to afford the materials, so that idea didn't pan out either."

Keith paused and pulled into the almost empty parking lot next to the old building.

"You hungry?"

"Yeah, I'm starved."

They were headed to Ma's, adjacent to the abandoned building.

"Anyways, since the hardware store made no money, it was changed into a restaurant. It didn't have much of a kitchen, only a small stove to cook, mainly, different types of stews and cornbread."

Keith held the glass-framed front door for Whitney. A cowbell hanging from the top of the steel doorframe jingled loudly. The dining room was small, but spacious. The tables had red-and-white-checkered tablecloths, and the hardwood floors were shiny. At the back there was a small stage, room for at most three people. Just to left of the stage a swinging door led to the kitchen.

It was eight-thirty. There were four old women sitting in one booth and a group of teenaged boys sitting in another. There were four big-bellied men dressed in work clothes at one of the middle tables. At the other, an old man sat reading a paper and sipping black coffee.

"How y'all doin' this mornin'?" Keith and Whitney heard from one of the waitresses while waiting at the door. She spoke fast and loudly. Dressed in red with a black waist apron, she was serving the lone old man his food.

"Just fine," Whitney replied.

The waitress moved a mile a minute around the dining room.

"As you can see we ain't too busy at the moment. Y'all can sit anywhere you'd like."

"Thank you, ma'am."

Keith smiled. His right arm gently caressed Whitney's lower back as they headed toward their booth next to the elderly ladies.

"What y'all drinking this-mo-nin'?"

"Two coffees with cream, no sugar, and a glass of orange juice."

"Well, all righty. Two coffees with cream and a glass of orange juice coming right up with a couple menus. My name's Missy. If y'all need a thing, just holler."

They sat in silence for a few minutes, casually watching the patrons of Ma's.

"So what did your grandpa do there on Sundays if everyone else was in church?"

"Come again?"

"Your grandpa. What'd he do in the restaurant? Was he a cook?"

"Oh … no, he cleaned up the place on Sunday mornings. Ended up, the restaurant wasn't too successful either. But on Friday and Saturday nights folks would come in and play music, dance, drink. That became popular real quick. Folks would come from miles away just to hear music, sometimes staying the night because it would be too late and far to return home. The owner wasn't too fond of that idea, but my grandpa convinced him to let them keep at it. He loved playing music. According to my ma and grandma he was *the* fiddle player, but he'd never admit it."

Missy arrived and gave Keith a quick glance. Her sweet southern accent was thick and had a unique drawl.

"Here you are."

Missy was in her early twenties. She was a niece of the owner of Ma's. She had a head full of blond and brownish locks. Her eyes appeared blue when she wore blue, and green when she wore green; if she wore any other color they looked gray. Her skin was caramel brown and tan from playing in the sun as a child, and her face burst with tiny freckles. Her dimples sat deep in her cheek.

"So where y'all from? Don't mean to be nosy, but we don't get too many visitors in this here small Alabama town."

"Uh-huh. Well, we're coming from North Carolina."

"Well, my my. What kind of business y'all got down here in little Pineapple?"

Whitney looked at Keith from across the table. He hadn't yet shown her much emotion toward Billy's death, and she was wondering how he'd react. Trying to ease some sort of pain that she thought held him, she leaned forward and reached to grab his hands. He appreciated her silent gesture, but didn't want others to see what might be construed as pity. That was the one thing he could not and would not tolerate: pity. As Whitney reached for him he casually moved his hands away and toward his creamers to prepare his coffee. Whitney's hands, defeated, went numb and lay flat on the table.

"Well, actually, I'm here to bury my brother."

Missy straightened her posture and her eyebrows rose.

"Oh."

There was a pause.

"Are you a Smith? I heard that a Smith boy died last week."

"No, ma'am, I'm a Baker."

"A Baker? I don't believe I know any Bakers. What was your brother's name?"

"His name was Billy. He died about a week ago."

Another brief pause filled the air. Only the clatter of dishes and chatting voices were heard.

"Well, I'm sorry to hear that."

"Oh, well, thank you," Keith said awkwardly. Missy was young, and death was a brash side note to her full life. Whitney saw Missy was a bit tongue-tied and discomforted. She gestured to the four big-bellied men.

"They didn't eat all the food, did they?"

Missy smiled.

"Naw, don't y'all worry none. We got plenty of food. I'll give y'all a few minutes and I'll be right back to take your order, okay?"

Missy hurried to the table of fat men to give them their checks. Whitney drank her orange juice. The pulp sat thick, so thick it could've been strained. Keith stirred his coffee with a small, silver teaspoon. He noticed the spoon had a coffee stain on it, but used it anyway. Cleanliness was a relative term, and he'd never understood why some people considered others dirty, when he knew everyone had their own soiled secrets, even his own self, he thought.

Keith thought for a moment and wished he hadn't told the young waitress about Billy. It wasn't shame he felt, but he dreaded the uneasiness he would feel when reintroduced to old acquaintances with questions about his whereabouts for the past twenty years. Whitney could always tell his mood by the look in his eyes, as could most people, even folks he'd just met. They sagged and sat deep, moving slowly, contemplating every detail. His hands, mimicking his eyes, fidgeted with the spoon, the saltshaker, and the napkin that lay under the fork and knife that Missy set.

"What are you thinking about?"

He looked from his coffee to meet her eyes. He wasn't going to tell her. He wasn't going to tell her how he'd missed this place for years, but was scared to return because of the bridges he'd burned or thought he'd burned.

"I think I forgot to close the barn door."

Whitney knew he was lying, but tolerated his speech. She'd lost too many relationships. The men in her life had never been comfortable expressing themselves, and she had tried to somehow get it out of them. They were stubborn, cold, hard. She had decided that it wasn't their entire fault; she was to blame as well. *Who had made me the confession booth?* she had finally thought to herself, disgusted with her unending drive to constantly know what her man was thinking. But with Keith she changed, or at least told herself that she had. She loved him too much to let him go. She'd decided she may never know what he was thinking, but she would love him for his consistency at manhood.

"Well, that's alright. Dale is always out and about, and you know if he sees anything he'll shoot it since he's always two sheets to the wind."

Keith grinned and let go of his contemplative mood.

There was a pause.

"You know what you're going to order?" Keith finally asked.

"A couple of biscuits, two scrambled eggs, and country ham. You?"

"I'm leaning toward some grits with cheese, eggs, and biscuits with gravy."

"This place smells so good, it just makes you more hungry."

"Welcome to 'Bama."

The room smelled of salty ham, fried bacon, and melted butter. Keith inhaled the scent that loomed like fog after a summer rain.

"You know, I think I'm gonna have to get country ham as well," Keith added.

Missy came through the swinging doors holding a pen in one hand and a small notepad in the other. Dan, the owner of Ma's, followed her. He glanced to the left and right, making sure his customers were occupied and content, and then continued following Missy. He was wearing blue jeans and a gray T-shirt that read, "Sweet Home Alabama." The shirt had an outlined sketch of Alabama with a banjo, fiddle, and guitar on the inside. A long, white apron filled with grease stains was tied to his waist and hung to his knees. Perspiration had soaked through and stained his armpits. His belly overlapped the apron, and his chest and shoulders were broad. He was an intimidating figure, but when he smiled he was warm, jovial, and at ease.

"Well, Lord of Mercy! Look what the cat done drug in."

The elderly ladies in the booth turned and giggled. The eyes of the lone man at the middle table rose from the paper he was reading and looked on, but the rest of his posture remained still and not amused.

Dan's banter continued.

"It must have been, shit, fifteen, twenty years. Missy said a man named Baker was sitting out here, but I swore she was mistaken. I had to come out and check for certain. I looked through them swinging doors and knew it was you. Keith, how the hell are you?"

Dan turned to Whitney, bowed, and without giving Keith a chance to respond, grabbed her hand with his two hands.

"Good day, ma'am. How are you?"

As the owner Dan considered it his duty to make his female customers feel at home. This usually entailed flirting, but to him it was merely southern hospitality. Keith didn't mind, as it was just that, southern hospitality—that soulful and mental freedom that resonated among the folk. Though pain of all sorts had certainly plagued this region of the South, their God still filled them with hope, a hope that shined bright and warm in common conversations.

Growing up with five older brothers, Whitney knew how men became overly flirtatious with their friend's significant others. She fluttered her eyelashes and gave the shy, innocent look of a schoolgirl. She replied with an aristocratic southern accent.

"I'm just fine, mister. How you today?"

Missy, standing behind Dan, giggled.

"Keith, she's a mighty fine looking. How'd you trick her into being with you?"

"Well, Dan, I found her up North. You know all the women is good-looking up there!"

"Shit. Well, I'll just have to stick with my two-toothed, tobacco-chewing, bearded wife, 'cause I'll be damned if you see me beyond these Alabama lines."

They laughed, like old friends. As the laughing fizzled away, Dan's face turned somber.

"Keith, I'm sorry to hear about old Billy. He was finally straightening up and then."

Keith cut him short.

"Thanks, Dan. Everything will be alright. We're going to bury him on Sunday morning at the old county cemetery. It'll just be a small and brief ceremony."

There was a pause and a sullen stare.

"Hmm, mmm. I apologize I can't attend. I'm going to the Smith's boy's funeral on Sunday."

There was a pause.

"I heard about that. Please give my regards to his family for me."

"Will do."

"Say, how are your folks doing?"

There was a pause. Dan sighed.

"You know Ma passed six years ago. And Pa, well, Pa's been gone for some time now."

Keith realized he'd put his foot in his mouth. He had received the news of both their deaths, but being away for so long he'd lost track of the deaths, births, and marriages. At least that was his rationalization. He was at a loss of words. All he said was, "Oh, I'm sorry. I didn't know." His eyes told another story.

There was a pause and a sullen stare.

"Sure. Well, you should come on down more often. What are you doing with yourself these days anyways?"

"I'm raising beef cattle up in North Carolina. Nothing too serious. Just something to put food on the table, occasionally. So, are you running this place?"

Dan looked around, content with his handiwork.

"Yes, sir. Ma opened this place after it burned down next door—that place your granddaddy worked. Anyway, after Ma died back in '82 I took it over. We don't make too much money, but it's a family affair. It was special to Ma, so I decided I'd do what I could to keep it going."

There was a pause.

Dan searched Keith's square face, the polished buttons on his plaid and ironed shirt, the neatly combed part in his hair, and the mole on his cheek just below his left sideburns, not knowing what he was looking for, but intent on finding it.

"Keith, now, you know, folks down here don't take family and community pride lightly. As you know. Or have you forgotten?"

The hospitality had begun to evaporate. Dan was proud of his courage for neither neglecting nor abandoning his home and his family. *Keith had done both*, Dan thought, an easy write-off for southern manhood. *Where had Keith been and why hadn't he returned?* Dan thought with growing animosity. Noticing the tension, Whitney interjected.

"Well, it's the finest-smelling restaurant I've ever stepped in."

"Well, much obliged, ma'am."

Keith knew Dan was right. He had abandoned Alabama. He had abandoned Billy and his roots. But Dan could never have understood that for Keith it took *his* leaving to understand how to find *his* home. This was hardly the norm for a southern gentleman.

"Y'all know any meal you take here'll be a free one."

"No, sir, Dan. I couldn't let you do that."

"That's the only way to do it."

Keith paused and glared a look of protest, but Whitney interjected once again.

"Thank you, Dan. That's mighty nice of you."

"Just a little southern hospitality for you Yankees. You know, someone told me just last week that 'damn' and 'yankee' was actually two words. Sho 'nuff. You know anything north of Birmingham is considered Yankee in these parts."

They laughed again, and Dan's teddy-bear persona resurrected.

"Thanks, Dan," Keith said.

"Don't mention it. Say, you know ol' Otis's working in the back?"

"Otis?"

"Yeah, ol' Otis Brown."

"OB from high school? No."

"Yes, sir. He's been the main cook since Ma was around."

Dan leaned forward, shielding his voice from the other patrons. Even Missy, who was right behind him, couldn't hear him.

"Y'all know niggers can cook like you ain't seen. Especially them from down these parts. Or have you forgotten?"

Dan laughed. Keith and Whitney grinned. Whitney bit her tongue and ignored her urge to interject a third time.

There was a pause.

"Tell Otis I said hello," Keith said.

"He'll be on out to holler at y'all after a while."

Dan retraced his steps to the kitchen and stopped at the old man's table to pick up an empty plate.

"Y'all ready to order?" Missy asked.

"I'd say so," Keith said.

As Missy wrote down Keith and Whitney's orders, she used her pen to comb back some of her blond locks that had escaped her ponytail. She left hurriedly to check on the other patrons.

Keith and Whitney sat in a comfortable silence, enjoying the southern ambience. The four big-bellied men finished and departed. The table of teen-aged boys was the loudest group. They told stories, laughed, and occasionally cursed, just loud enough to raise an onlooking eyebrow. The lone man sitting in the middle was still fixated on his paper. He had a wooden walking stick that lay across an empty seat. It was hand carved of a hard wood. At the end it was circularly curved, like a stick-shift handle, easy to grip.

"Who's Otis Brown?" Whitney asked.

There was a pause.

Keith took another long sip from his coffee.

"I went to school with Otis. He was the only black student at our school. We were only a class of thirty-five, and the entire school didn't have more than seventy-five kids."

"Weren't there other black kids and families?"

"In the area, sure, but they all attended the school for the blacks about ten or so miles from here."

"So why didn't he go there?"

"Well, there's a story to it. Otis's father, Kati, was a highly respected man by both whites and blacks. He was like the black's representative, so to speak. He was educated, well spoken, and fearless. If the blacks were mistreated or weren't given proper rights to their own land to grow crops, they'd go to Kati for help. Kati would go directly to the white folks to discuss what was going on. He's a bit of a legend, as was his father, Unk. He was completely honest with the white folks, usually the men, the white men. They always listened to what he'd say and usually matters improved. You know, growing up here, I always heard old men talk about Otis's grandfather Unk and they said it was never what he said, but how he said it. More still, it was how he looked. They said his eyes seemed to look straight through you. Otis's father, Kati, had a similar effect on folks."

"His name was Unk?"

"Yes, ma'am. I can't recall how he got that name, but that's how everyone knew him. Just Unk. Anyways, one day Otis came home from the black school—grade ten, I think—and he said they didn't have any books, no materials, even the walls seemed to be falling apart. Apparently, everything had been taken out and given to a newly repaired white school in a neighboring county. So Kati went to the principal of Pine Blossom High and asked him if Otis could attend. At first the principal refused, but after a week Otis started coming to school. It was rumored that Mr. Jones was afraid of Kati and had terrible nightmares for a whole week after seeing him. I guess no one really knows, but anyways, Otis was real shy, but he was by far the hardest-working student. He got better grades than all of us, but graduated number thirty-five."

"How'd that happen?"

"Kati died two months before graduation and coincidentally Otis dropped from valedictorian to number thirty-five."

That was all Keith wanted to tell Whitney. Maybe he'd tell her the rest someday: how Kati was shot while picking cotton one day in the fields, and how Otis was beaten every day in the bathrooms and hallways at school, and of the close, but distant, bond that he and Otis developed during their two years of schooling together. Keith thought that was all that needed to be told, because if he continued, he would only sound like a storyteller, merely an onlooker and not part of the action. He didn't think himself the same Keith from these stories he was telling of his past.

"Well, here y'all are."

Missy had arrived with their plates of food, a couple of bowls—one with peach jelly, the other with homemade apple butter—and the steaming pot of coffee. She topped off their mugs and told Keith that Otis would be out momentarily.

Their hunger deterred their conversation. Whitney's eyes scanned her plate searching for the best starting point. She grabbed one of the biscuits, sliced it, and placed a slab of country ham on one side and two forks full of scrambled eggs. The other side she smothered with apple butter and made a sandwich. Keith slopped the grits atop his sunny-side-up eggs and forked a piece of country ham on top, saving the biscuits and gravy for the dessert. They ate in silence, perfectly content and distracted from the dining room scenery.

Otis approached. Whitney was still chewing as he greeted Keith. She casually put her napkin to cover her face as she had just shoved a huge bite of her biscuit sandwich in her mouth.

"Howdy, stranger," Otis said.

Otis's outfit looked similar to Dan's: jeans, white apron, sweaty T-shirt. But their builds differed. Otis was slim and muscular. He had wide forearms with thick, bulging veins. There was a long and chiseled scar that ran from his right collarbone to his jawbone. Otis wore an old, faded, and brown baseball cap that was tightly folded, and which read "Budweiser."

"Otis, how you doin'?"

Keith smiled and reached to shake his hand. Otis reciprocated. His eyes stood still and hidden under his low-fitted hat. His voice was deep and deliberate.

"I'm doing just fine. Ma'am, how are you doing this morning?"

Behind them the old ladies in the booth whispered.

"I'm doing fine. You cook a mighty fine breakfast."

"I'm glad you're enjoying it. I see you've turned it into lunch with that sandwich."

Whitney grinned.

"Otis, how's Pineapple?"

"Keith, you know Pineapple ain't ever going to change. But it's home. Say, I'm sorry to hear about Billy," Otis said with a straight, but tender face. He looked Keith directly in his eyes.

"Thanks, Otis. He was finally straightening up," Keith started.

Otis cut him short.

"Keith, you don't have to explain. Man lives and dies. There ain't no words that can really say more than that."

There was a pause.

Keith was flustered, hesitant, meek. His mind wondered. His words had always been chosen carefully, but he was now at a loss for words. He wanted to cry out and say things that had never been heard from him before.

Whitney noticed Keith was anxious and disheartened. Otis continued, unaffected.

"Listen, y'all. I got to get back to this here kitchen, otherwise Dan may burn down the joint."

Otis lowered toward Keith and Whitney to whisper.

"You know, white folk can't cook nohow."

They chuckled, then smiled. Otis continued.

"I reckon it's last minute, but y'all come on over this evening—say about seven or eight."

"Oh, Otis, you know," Keith started.

Otis cut Keith short.

"Don't even try it. Naw, sir. We live on down by Gullie's River. You remember them houses that was down there, don't you?"

"How could I forget them?"

"Well, we at 5211—just off the river."

Whitney smiled. Otis looked to her and smiled.

"So, who's we?" Keith asked.

"Myself, wife, and kids. You'll see them soon enough. I'll be seeing y'all."

Otis turned and walked toward the swinging door. The old man at the middle table still sat and read his newspaper, and the country ham still filled the air of Ma's dining room.

THE FIVE-STRING

"I ain't think you'd forget the way."

Otis hollered to Keith as he and Whitney approached the front porch. It was dark, just past eight o'clock. In Pineapple the Alabama night sky was always crisp and clear—even during the muggy and moist months. The moon was full and bright, like a flashlight; the stars had not yet begun to shine. Fireflies rippled through the thick but breezy air.

Keith and Whitney walked to the wide cemented porch where three wooden rocking chairs sat. Wooden white posts held the overhanging roof, which sagged slightly. Otis sat in the lone rocker to the right of the front door. His head leaned against the back headrest, and his long legs were stretched out in front of him. He was much more relaxed than when Keith had seen him earlier in the morning.

The screen porch door kept mosquitoes out of the house. Soft, yellow light from the house lit the porch. The night was still, but wary of critters. Nina Simone, singing the blues, exuded from the house. Whitney's brown curls shone in the moonlight.

"How could I forget this little town? There ain't but four or five paved streets," Keith said.

"And you know they won't even paved until five years ago," Otis responded, grinning.

They firmly shook hands and memories pulsated their palms.

"It's real good to see you, Otis," Keith said.

"Yeah, it's been awhile."

There was a pause.

Otis glanced at Whitney's garb—a white linen and cotton dress cut just to her shins.

"You look mighty nice this evening, ma'am."

The deepness of Otis's tone in his speech was rhythmic, seductive even.

"Lawd, lawd, these southern men have a way with words," Whitney said, blushing.

They laughed.

"Won't y'all have a seat? I'll get Krista."

Keith and Whitney sat. Otis went through the front door. The sound of his footsteps echoed from the heels of his shoes, and the smell of fried cooking and boiling potatoes passed through the air.

The flow of the creek hummed behind the house. To the right, a lone light shined on the porch. To the left, two rugged children wrestled in the moonlight and a growling puppy playfully watched. Across the road there was a shallow area of tall pines. Behind them was an open field of crops—corn, millet, beans, and cabbage.

The grass shined. The natural music of the landscape—the swaying crops, the shining moon, the waving grass—harmonized with the human-ized sounds of the harmonica, the snare drum, the fiddle bass, and Nina wailing on the microphone.

Keith was trying to remember Otis as he knew him in the past. He was a shy classmate, but he was confident and strong. Keith was anxious to find out who Otis had become.

"It's humid out," Whitney said.

"Oh, yeah. But this isn't real humid. Now, June, July, August. Shoo-wee, talk about being humid. You step outside and just sweat standing still. There's usually a late afternoon shower, but after it, it's just as muggy."

There was a pause.

"Have you met Otis's wife?"

"No. You know, I haven't seen him in at least twenty-five or so years. I haven't been down this road in … well, probably longer."

Otis's footsteps echoed back through to the front of the house. He held the front porch screen for the woman and the two little boys who followed; in one hand he grasped a brown envelope.

"Keith, this is my wife Krista."

Krista's skin tone was light brown, like caramel. Her rosy cheeks were wide and her dimples accentuated an attractive chubbiness in her face. She wore light maroon lipstick that looked wet on her lips. Her eyes held wrinkles, but she didn't look old. The lines were the markings of long days and little sleep; her eyes moved with ease and excitement. Her hair was twisted and tied in dreadlocks that fell to her shoulder blades. The snug sheath dress that hung to her shins revealed her muscular arms and shoulders. Her breasts stood firm and looked heavy.

Keith smiled to Krista, and he held out his hand to her.

"Nice to meet you, Keith."

Their hands embraced.

"So, you used to live in these parts?" Krista asked.

"Yes, ma'am. Well, many years ago."

Krista exuded warmth.

"Krista, this is Whitney," Keith said.

The two women smiled and greeted one another. Their beauty was clear as the moon. As they made small talk, the smaller of the two boys wrapped his arms around Krista's leg and peered up at the white strangers. He was at the age of pure innocence—not jaded by the lewd looks that folks of different races, cultures, and economic classes were prone to pass. Eyes, mouths, and noses were what interested him the most. He briefly looked to Keith, but was in awe of Whitney. He pulled on Krista's dress while staring at her with his mouth slightly ajar. The other boy, a few years older, stood behind Otis. He occasionally and hesitantly lifted his head to look at the visitors and to the children next door.

"Keith, Whitney, these are our children," Otis said.

Otis put his hand on the older boy's head, palming it.

"This is JR. He's seven."

Otis put the brown envelope in his back pocket and picked up the smaller boy, who neglected to speak. His eyes were fixated on Whitney in toddler wonderment.

"And this is Shawn, but we call him Lilunk. He's three. Can y'all say 'good evening' to these folks?"

Otis, the father, spoke in a calm but demanding tone. The older boy lowered his head and began.

"Good evening, sir."

"Boy, pick your head up when you speak," Otis said, sharply cutting off JR.

JR quickly raised his head and looked to Keith's eyes. Keith saw a glimpse of the younger Otis he knew growing up.

"Good evening, sir."

"Howdy, JR. How are you?"

"Fine."

JR then greeted Whitney. With a mother's warmth, Krista gently caressed the boy's head.

"Good evening, JR. You surely do have nice manners," Whitney replied.

"Thank you, ma'am."

The small boy sat comfortably in Otis's arms, glancing back and forth to Keith and Whitney. His mouth was still ajar and his eyes blinked slowly. Keith attempted to shake hands with little Shawn, but the toddler became aware of the foreign face and began to cry. Whitney said that Keith often had that effect on people. At ease, they all laughed.

"JR, take Lilunk and put him to bed. You do your homework?" Otis asked.

JR softly replied.

"Huh? Speak up."

"Yes, sir."

"Alright then, go on to bed."

Otis kissed both boys on their heads and handed Lilunk to his brother, who carried him as best he could.

"Good night, JR, Lilunk," Whitney whispered as the boys walked through the door.

"Otis, didn't you say you had three kids?" Keith asked.

"Yes, sir. The third is our daughter Ebony. She's just three months old," Otis replied.

Krista interjected.

"She's already been fed. She's been asleep an hour or so. But don't worry. She'll be up crying before too long. Whitney, dinner's almost ready. You want to help me finish up, and we'll give these boys a chance to catch up?"

"Sure."

Krista led Whitney into the kitchen. The men took their seats on the rocking chairs.

"Say, Keith. Before I forget, here's a letter for you."

He grabbed the brown envelope from his back pocket and handed it to Keith.

"I wrote this just after you left Pineapple back in '65, a few months after Bloody Sunday. I won't sure where you went. I'd heard Pensacola, Mobile, somewhere in Tennessee maybe. So I held on to it."

Keith looked at the permanent creases. It was addressed to him, to some address at the University of Alabama. Keith figured it was his dormitory address, but he could hardly recall it. The envelope had a two-cent stamp of the American flag on it. It also had been marked, "RETURNED: NON-EXISTING RESIDENT."

"Finally I heard from Mr. Sloan at the swap meet you was at school at the university so I mailed it. Two or three months later it was returned. At that point I figured I'd hold on to it, thinking I'd see you some time."

"You probably didn't think it'd be this long."

"No, sir."

Keith went to open it, but Otis stopped him.

"Just hold on to it. I don't really remember what's on them lines. It might be embarrassing for the both of us."

"Alright. I reckon I can write back."

Otis nodded, but they both knew there would be no reply, no response. Not many in Pineapple knew where he went. Keith often left personal matters undone, as he had left Pineapple never to return, as he left Timothy Simon sitting on the maroon Persian rug on that cold February morning to move to the farm in Esmont. Keith would only return on his terms, when it was convenient for him. He slipped the letter in his back pocket.

Krista came out holding two glasses.

"Sweet tea, gentlemen?"

"Thank you, ma'am," Keith responded.

"Thanks, baby," Otis said.

She returned to the house just as quickly as she had come out.

"How long y'all been married?" Keith asked.

"We been married about fifteen years. Mmm, yeah, fifteen years next February. But she ain't my first wife. My first kids, but she ain't my first wife."

"Krista's number two?"

"A couple of years after high school I got married to Chantel Williams from North Wilcox. You ain't know her, I don't think. Her family and my family were close friends. Our mothers always joked about us getting hitched when we was young. In high school we started secretly dating and finally I asked her hand in marriage. My uncles was irate, saying I was too young, but I'd caught the bug and didn't care. The first year was good, but the next two were too damn much. Too much family. People knowing every thing, or at least thinking they did. We won't getting along real well and she couldn't get pregnant. Money was tight. Finally I had to step back, get out. I'd gone to Shreveport, Louisiana, to work with a cousin at a paper mill factory. I left, and a couple months later she wanted a divorce. They won't much paperwork involved because we ain't have nothing, just had to sign some papers here and there."

There was a pause.

The men sipped the sweet tea. The stars began to poke the covers of the night sky.

"How'd you and Krista meet?"

"She lived in Shreveport. She was a teacher for night school students at the mostly black community college there. They called it a college, but a degree from there didn't mean much. Anyways, I took a couple of classes, thinking I'd someday get a chance at university. She taught African American history. I won't even enrolled in the class, but sat in because she was something else to set eyes upon. She was fine. Still is. All them knuckleheads didn't give a damn about the class—neither did I. They'd just hoped and prayed she'd wear a shorter skirt or a revealing blouse the next night in class.

"Anyways, one night an assignment was due and since I won't even in the class I ain't turn nothing in. She noticed and asked me about it. I didn't want to tell her the truth, so I kept giving her stories. Finally, she told me to stay after class. I won't even thinking about trying to get with her then. I was scared of her. She could've talked me in circles, confusing me with words I ain't know. But she was nice. We talked. I told her the truth. One thing led to another, and we got married a couple years later."

"Just like that, huh? So, how'd y'all get back to Pineapple?"

"After Ma died I told Krista I couldn't leave this place, even though my mind may of wanted to. She told me that anything I wanted to do, we'd do together. Now, that's love, brother. So we came down here. We ain't rich by no means, but we got plenty: work, food on the table. Now we got three kids."

There was a pause.

The men continued to sip their sweet tea. The mother of the boys playing in the yard next door yelled to them to come into the house.

"Lord, that's a story," Keith said.

"It ain't been easy to live."

The children next door ran inside, leaving the yelping puppy on the porch. The crickets were louder and the air thickened.

"You been married?" Otis asked.

Keith sighed sullenly.

"Yeah, I've been married."

Otis snickered.

"Uh-oh. Sounds like you been divorced, too," he said.

Keith chuckled.

"Yeah," he said.

"So we're both one-for-two."

"Well, no, sir. I'm oh-for-one."

They laughed.

"Women! Damn, man, women! You mean, you and Whitney ain't married?"

"No, sir."

"But you're thinking about it? That's a fine woman."

"Yes, sir, but I don't want to go zero-for-two."

They laughed.

"Man, you can go zero-for-twelve, but still hit a homerun," Otis said.

"You know that gets expensive, though?"

"Sho 'nuff."

They laughed.

"You got children?" Otis asked.

"Yes, sir. One son."

"What's your son's name?"

"Timothy Simon."

The air thickened even more, tightening the throats of Otis and Keith, like an overachieving Sunday Windsor knot.

"Y'all got a good relationship—you and your son?"

"I'd like to think so, but I don't always know."

"Oh, come on, now, I'm sure you do. Do he live with you?"

"No. He lives with his mom about four and a half hours away. We see each other on long weekends and sometimes during holidays. Otis, you know our lives are in two different worlds. He's in school, in the city. I'm on a farm, staying away from city life."

There was a pause.

Crickets broke the silence.

"But, you know, Keith, there ain't but one world."

Otis was a humble man, as was Keith, but their humble demeanors came out in different ways. Otis was openly proud, but only because in his heart and soul he was certainly blessed from afar; Otis recognized and deeply appreciated his blessings. Keith was easily reserved, keenly observant, and unemotional, but quietly clever, oftentimes too much so for his own good.

"Yes, sir. I reckon, Otis, that's true."

Keith was apprehensive to share his thoughts, his feelings, and his frustrations with fatherhood. He preferred to sit reserved and silent. Keith appreciated Otis's humble yet proud demeanor and thought about Otis's grandfather Unk. He was certain that attribute was one passed through strong bloodlines. JR and Lilunk would offer the world the same humility. Keith thought about his own blood—Timothy Simon. What did his bloodline leave his son? Keith thought. He questioned why his son didn't understand him. Was it his reserved disposition? he wondered.

It was Keith's silence. Timothy Simon was at an age eager to define himself. His changing physical and psychological self demanded confrontation. He hadn't lived long enough to know more. His father, the imposing but absent figure, was not worth the confrontation, in Timothy Simon's eyes. He resented his father for his seemingly selfish and distancing quietude. Keith, the father, was there for the celebrations and holidays, but during the day-to-day adolescent struggles Timothy Simon experienced, his father was absent and silent; their relationship was dormant. Timothy took his father's silence for want of care, want of love. Timothy Simon, as yet, had not the words to articulate his feelings toward his father. His feelings came out in the form of angry temperament and misdirected language, like, "I hate," and "I wish he wasn't my father." Keith didn't know Timothy Simon used these words of disregard, but could feel the tension between them. Yet he was apprehensive to respond. *Where did the roads of father and child meet?* Keith thought.

There was a pause.

Tree frogs by the creek began to croak, and a lone owl in the tall pines across the road began to hoot.

The two men occasionally made small talk, but they mostly sat in a comfortable silence, rocking. Subconsciously they were feeling the waters of their revisited camaraderie. Memories from a shared past resurfaced, but the passing of time anchored their eagerness at conversation.

"Y'all boys had enough talking?" Whitney asked as she approached the porch.

"Yes, ma'am." Otis replied.

"Mmm...mmm. I'm ready to eat," Keith said.

The air was immediately cooler when they stepped in the house. The trees surrounding the houses in the area were an efficient source of shade. Later in the night, however, the heavy air would permeate through the walls. The Alabama night air cannot be tamed.

The living room looked larger from the inside than from out. The floors were hardwood, but were so dark and worn the lines separating the panels of wood were barely visible. The living room was divided into two parts by a walkway through the house that led to the kitchen. On the sun-setting side a television sat catty-cornered by the wall. Diagonal to the television there was a brown leather La-Z-Boy recliner, Otis's royal throne. A three-cushion sofa, comfortably worn and decorated in different shades of green, sat next to the recliner. In front of it there was a long wooden coffee table carved with typical West African décor.

To the left of the walkway there was a dark brown and leather sofa. In the corner there was an old, black woodstove. A wide vinyl mat decorated with yellow daises lay underneath the stove to protect the hardwood floor. It was common for homes in southern Alabama to have woodstoves in the main living area. Before television and radio, cooking was the main attraction, and it was considered central heating for the brisk but snowless winters.

A dim overhead light lit the living room. The walls were light brown.

Framed pictures of family and friends lined the walls. Keith was drawn to an old banjo that hung above the green sofa. The strings were loose and dusty. Keith couldn't quite identify it, but it looked familiar. He was certain he had seen that exact banjo somewhere before.

"Otis, you play?" Keith asked.

Otis turned to Keith.

"Ah, I tried to some years back."

"You know, maybe I'm wrong, but I swear I've seen this banjo before somewhere."

"I'm sure you have. This here banjo's a popular item."

"Yeah, I reckon most are. But, no, I mean not any banjo, this banjo. I know I've seen it before."

"I know. And I know you have. Like I said, this here banjo's a popular item."

"I declare, I knew it. Otis, where've I seen this before?

"Well, not in this house, here. Probably your granddaddy's house when you was a kid."

"Well, I'll be. I reckon. Is that? But how do you have it?"

Otis grinned and brushed the dusty and sooty strings.

"Shit," he said softly. "I need to tune this here. And I need to clean it up."

Keith couldn't place it from his memory. It had been too many years, and trying to remember Pineapple was like reinventing it.

"Otis, it's been too long," Keith said.

"You don't remember?"

"No, sir. I reckon I don't."

"Your granddaddy gave this banjo to my granddaddy Unk after he helped him in the sharecropper's fight with the land owner."

"You mean to Big Unk?"

"Yeah, to Big Unk."

"But. Really? You know. I can't recall that. What happened?"

Otis laughed.

"Ah, man. Keith, you have been gone a long time. You don't remember?"

"No, sir."

"Well, it's too long a story for me to tell you. Ask Pastor Johnson tomorrow. He's doing Billy's funeral right?"

"Hmm-mmm."

"Yeah, you should ask about it tomorrow."

"Alright, but, Otis, you can't."

Otis interjected.

"Naw, man. Hear it from him. Hear it from him. Come on now, let's eat."

Keith laughed and sighed. He was anxious to rekindle the story of his people. "Alright."

Otis turned and walked to the dining room. It was an intimate house. The open rooms fluidly led to one another, as did its occupants and the occupants from generations past, who were all linked by blood, tears, and joy.

The four ate fried toast, baked chicken, mashed potatoes, green beans, corn on the cob, and peach cobbler. They ate like old friends, told stories, and laughed. The intimacy of the house had a relaxing effect on them.

As they ate dessert Ebony cried in the background. Krista went to feed her and later carried her out in her arms. Ebony was tiny, light-skinned, and fragile. She sat quietly in Krista's arms. Whitney asked to hold the infant, and Krista brought Ebony to her. Krista warmly passed her child, her blood, to Whitney.

As the evening came to an end Otis and Keith shook hands, as firmly as before, and Krista and Whitney hugged. Otis and Keith exchanged contact information. Keith asked Otis to visit him in North Carolina, but they knew if they met again it would only be in Pineapple. Keith, anxious to remember the story of the banjo, forgot about the brown envelope in his back pocket.

B.J. Baker

The headstone had not yet arrived. Keith had to make the final payment to Addie May Collins Cemetery Monuments. It wouldn't be planted until after the funeral and then the casket burial. It was a simple stone that read, "Billy Joe Baker, October 20, 1946–November 15, 1990." Underneath B.J.'s name and dates of birth and death there read the fourteenth verse of the thirteenth chapter of the book of Romans: "Rather, clothe yourselves with the Lord Jesus Christ, and do not think about how to gratify the desires of the sinful nature." Pastor Johnson selected the verse. It wasn't particularly appropriate for B.J., but no one voiced this concern or opinion. It was a part of the cemetery, like the neatly trimmed grass and the intricate flowerbeds. It was merely part of the routine of death in this southern Alabama town.

The casket was wide and long, much larger than the size of B.J. Keith doubted Billy's living bed had been as roomy or as comfortable. On each side of the length of the hardwood casket there were three handles, but there hadn't been six able carriers at the funeral. After the service the casket was wheeled to the hearse.

Keith noticed the intricate design of the casket. All of the trouble to construct this casket, all the time it took to carve and properly polish the dome-top shape, seemed almost ridiculous. It had been made to be buried. *Were people made to die, too?* he thought.

Billy was buried at the Pine Forest Cemetery. It was a small cemetery in Wilcox County, near Pineapple. Many Bakers had been buried there, but they were scattered throughout the two-acre brick fenced lot. Some years back the funeral service of a Baker was more of an intimate experience. All the community attended—black and white. Families ate and prayed together.

On that November day, the sky was gray. Six people stood around the uprooted and dark brown earth. Pastor Johnson was at the head of the hole. Keith and Whitney stood to one side. Whitney wore a black V-neck dress with the sleeves cut at her biceps. Atop it she wore a gray, light sweater jacket her mother had knitted for her. Hanging from her neck was a silver necklace with a simple cross charm.

Across from Whitney and Keith stood Daffney Smith—the woman who called Keith with the news of his brother's death—and her mother-in-law. Daffney was a childhood friend. Their families lived close to one another, and their fathers hunted deer together throughout the Wilcox County pine forests.

Daffney's mother-in-law was old and brittle. She grasped Daffney by her side as if she were a life jacket. She looked closer to death than B.J. was in his own casket. Static from her faded purple dress clung to her thighs. The thick pantyhose painted her skin tone a shade darker; however, her deep varicose veins soaked through. Her wrinkled lips held a slow-burning cigarette. Her lips didn't move; they merely inhaled the toxic smoke. The cigarette was her respirator.

Keith watched the old hag with disgusted amusement. The gently rising fumes reminded Keith of Billy's smoking habits. Keith figured Billy started smoking when he was eight or nine years old; Keith was ten. One day after school they were walking home through the woods with a couple of other boys. Billy had stolen a pack of cigarettes from Mr. Bell, the math and science teacher. Billy wasn't sure what he was going do with them.

"I dare you to smoke 'em," one of the boys said.

Billy couldn't be outdone.

"One? Shit, that ain't nothin'," he retorted.

"Then smoke them all, pussy," Keith snapped.

"What'll you give me if I do?"

"I'll do your morning chores for two weeks."

"Nope."

"What, then?"

Billy thought for a moment, then said, "Y'all three got to shave your heads."

"Do what?"

"Y'all three have to shave your heads, bare and bald, if I smoke all these here cigarettes."

They thought it was a funny bet, but were sure Billy couldn't smoke all of the cigarettes.

"Alright, bitch, but you ain't gonna smoke them all, nohow," the boys said, challenging Billy.

They agreed to it, shook hands, and the bet was official. They all sat down and Billy smoked the full pack, right there in the forest, right in a row. Not surprisingly, he threw up, and threw up some more, but he won the bet. Later that same night, through his vomiting fits, Billy shaved his brother's head and the following morning he shaved the other two boys' heads. The next day at school everyone wanted to know why their heads were shaved, but the three knew that if they told, Billy would get into trouble. So they just said they had lost a bet. It didn't take much to figure what was wrong with Billy. He couldn't eat for two days and coughed like he had emphysema. Somehow the truth eventually leaked. It took a whole day and a half. Billy's homeroom teacher beat him at school, and then his mother and father beat him at home. Billy's parents were more upset with him stealing from Mr. Bell than him consuming the cigarettes. Thus began his thirty-six years of smoking. At least, Keith learned a lesson. He never smoked. He'd watched and heard his grandfather painfully cough, as well as his uncles and great uncles, and never had the desire to smoke.

Just behind and to the right of the old woman another woman stood. Keith didn't recognize the woman. Wife? No. Child? No, Billy had neither, so far as Keith knew. She was some twenty years Billy's younger, Keith guessed. She wore a black skirt that was seductively short for a funeral. Her face glistened with makeup, and her bangs were curled high above her forehead.

Pastor Johnson interrupted Keith's thoughts and straying eyes.

"Keith, would you like to say a few words?"

"Uh, no, sir. No, thank you."

Pastor Johnson then opened the floor to the four other attendees. The young woman stepped forward, high heels pounding. She pranced to the feet of Billy's casket where Whitney and Keith stood. She hugged Whitney, as if Whitney was her next-of-kin. She turned to Keith and planted a kiss right on his lips and then hugged him. Her lipstick was smeared on his bottom lip. She walked around to the head of the casket where Pastor Johnson stood and kissed him as well, leaving a mark on his cheek.

"Well, gosh, I don't know where to start," she began. "Y'all probably don't know me. I surely don't know y'all, but you seem, well, right nice. I'm Doloris. Doloris Evan Gumphrey from Jackson, Mississippi. I met B.J. when I was twenty-one. I'm twenty-six now. We met in the state penitentiary of Alabama in Birmingham. B.J. was in for, what was it, maybe, three months? I was on my first duty as a parole officer, and B.J. became my client. He was sweet as could be from the start. I was so lucky to have such a nice and respectful felon. He was released and given a fourteen-month parole. In those fourteen months we was only supposed to meet once a week, but we ended up meeting more often than that. Much more often."

The long-hanging ash from the old woman's cigarette fell.

"After them fourteen months, which, by the way, he completed perfectly, never failed a piss test or alcohol test, we moved in together. Or I reckon he moved in with me. We lived together for eight months. After that he said he had to come on home to take care of some business. Well, he left. It was a sad time for us both. Shortly after he left I got pregnant. And I really did think he was the father. After the creep who actually is the father, I sure wish B.J. *was* the real father. We ain't never lived together after that, but he still came to visit me whenever he'd pass through on I-95. Y'all must known he was a truck driver, right? I loved B.J., and I'm very sad he died."

She began to cry. Pastor Johnson gave her the white handkerchief from his back pocket. Doloris thanked him and blew her nose. The sound was deafening. Daffney began to cry, but the old woman was motionless. Keith was flabbergasted, almost to the point of hilarity, by Doloris's story. Whitney held Keith's arm.

"I didn't want to start doing this, but, well, I just loved him," Doloris started again.

She sobbed. Pastor Johnson looked to Keith to give him another chance to speak, but he refused.

∽

That night Keith and Whitney ate at Pastor Johnson's house. He lived in the house next to Pineapple Baptist, the only church in Pineapple. Pastor Johnson had grown up in that house, as had his father and grandfather, who were pastors, as well. Pastor Johnson's great-grandfather was never ordained as a preacher, but built the house and the church.

Pastor Johnson was the local historian for Pineapple. Church was a significant part of everyone's life, and whenever events occurred, folks would report it to the church, where it was recorded and filed. The first Johnson thought town recording was of the utmost importance. His strict adherence to recording these events passed on through the generations, as had his strong belief in Christ. Pastor Johnson could tell you exactly how many deaths and baptisms there were in 1850 and show you the files to prove it. It was no surprise to Keith that Otis would tell him to ask Pastor Johnson about the five-string banjo hanging on his wall.

Pastor Johnson had been married to a sweet lady named Bessy. She had died some twenty years ago. Keith didn't attend the funeral, but fondly remembered Mrs. Johnson. She was a robust and hefty woman, but so young and energetic. She always had gifts for Keith and Billy when they were younger, even if one of them was merely stopping to say hello on the way home from school. Often the gift was money—sometimes a dime, a quarter, and on special occasions a dollar. She'd also give gifts, like clothes and school supplies. As a child Keith figured she'd given every kid a gift. He thought it was her duty since she was the preacher's wife.

Later Keith realized she was so generous because they were so poor. The Great Depression hurt many families in the South. The Bakers lost plenty and never recovered. They lost most of their land, livestock, even had to move from their farmhouse into a undersized, three-room home. They surely weren't the only family living poorly, but Keith's mother was an active member of the church and one of Bessy's closest friends. They had grown up together and were like sisters. She had given gifts, as if she were Keith and Billy's aunt.

When Billy was fourteen, he and a couple of his friends went to the Johnsons' house and robbed Mrs. Bessy Johnson, or at least they tried to rob her. It was in December on the night of Christmas Eve. There were two services on Christmas Eve—one in the morning and one at night. Bessy always attended the morning service so that during the night service she and a handful of other wives could remain at home and cook and prepare the annual Christmas Eve meal that would be served to the deacons, ushers, altar boys and girls, and choir members. It just so happened that during that year, the same year Billy and two of his friends tried to rob these cooking women, Billy's mother was actually helping with the cooking.

The delinquents dressed in all black. Over their faces they wore ski masks. Only their eyes showed, but when they entered the house, which smelled of homemade cooking and was never locked, they put on sunglasses to hide their eyes.

They had been planning this outing for three or four weeks. Jeremy Keaton was the boy who was going to do the talking. Billy couldn't since Bessy would have easily recognized his voice. The boys entered the home and slowly shut all the blinds in the living room area. They cut off all the porch lights. The women were chatting in the kitchen and couldn't hear any noises from the other rooms. The boys rushed to the kitchen, and Jeremy ordered the women to get in the living room and lie down on their stomachs. These women were hard-working country folk who weren't scared of hoodlums. Knowing that, however, these boys held BB guns in their jacket pockets and threatened to shoot them if they spoke or did something out of line. Billy and these boys probably would've gotten away with it had it not been for Billy's mother who, at the time of the mad rush to the kitchen, was in the bathroom in a side hallway opposite the kitchen.

After the women did as they were told, Jeremy ordered Bessy to go with Danny, the other boy, to the safe in the master bedroom down the hallway to get all the money. Jeremy watched the women lying on the floor while Billy kept watch outside, just at the corner of the porch so he could see the church where most of the community would be. While Billy's mother was in the bathroom, however, she heard all that was said. When the time was just right, she snuck out of the bathroom and tiptoed to the kitchen. From the hallway she saw the women lying on the ground and Jeremy anxiously watching them and peering through the window. Billy's mother only thought there were two boys; little did she know her son was outside as the lookout man. In one swift and quiet movement she darted out through the kitchen door, picking up a frying pan on the way. As she stepped outside she heard the loud preaching of Pastor Johnson and thought to run for help. Then another voice, one quiet, close, and a bit too familiar, made her stop and listen.

"Shit. Fuck. Hurry this shit up. God damn it, Jeremy."

It was Billy, frantically looking back and forth to the church and inside the house from the side of the porch. He was too nervous to direct his attention to the side of the house, since all the action was happening inside of it.

After a second thought Billy's mother knew it was her troubled son. She slyly stood against the outside wall that ran to the corner of the porch where Billy stood. She could hear him talking to himself again and figured with all the lights out, Billy couldn't hear or see her.

"Come on now, Jeremy. . . . Come on now," Billy said to himself in anguish.

Billy's mother approached within reaching distance and stopped.

"Psst . . . psst . . . Billy," she whispered.

Billy stood stone cold. Her voice was too real to be true. He poked his head around the porch corner and whispered.

"Mom?"

WHAM.

Billy's mother gave a backhand swing with the frying pan and clubbed Billy directly in the face. His nose broke in two places, but that wasn't determined until he woke up. The hit left him unconscious for three hours. He had an unpleasant Christmas Day.

After, Billy's mother dropped her frying pan and ran to the church for help. When Jeremy and Danny exited the house they spotted Billy lying down with blood flowing down his face.

"Fuck. Billy?" Jeremy said, scrambling for answers.

"Son of a bitch," said Danny. "A fucking frying pan?"

The boys ran, but didn't get far. Three different groups of men formed the search party entourage. The men swept the cornfields and found them in the Newton's fields about a quarter of a mile from the church. Jeremy and Danny were beaten and dragged back to the Johnsons' home to apologize and to return the $65.37 that they had taken.

This would be Billy's first of several attempted robbery cases, only this one never went to court.

The Five-String Retold

"Could you please pass the milk, Pastor Johnson?" Whitney asked.

"Please, ma'am, call me 'Larry.'"

In Keith's forty-six years, he had seldom heard anyone call Pastor Johnson "Larry." He was always just "Pastor Johnson," to everyone except his wife Bessy, who called him "L.J."

Whitney, Keith, Pastor Johnson, and his granddaughter Valerie, who was in her mid-twenties, had just finished dinner and were sipping coffee and eating the apple pie that Valerie had made. Valerie was a surgical nurse for an ophthalmologist in Mississippi, but decided to move in with her grandfather to care for him. He was getting older and wasn't as able to do as much as he could in the past. For Valerie, it was important for her to be with him; he was her favorite and last living grandparent.

Valerie was beautiful and spunky, full of energy and excitement. She was also deaf. Pastor Johnson and Whitney both knew sign language. Whitney had learned to sign when she was a kid since her childhood friend was deaf. They translated for Keith. Pastor Johnson was a big tease with his grand-daughter Valerie. When they were discussing Keith's cow business, Valerie signed a question. Pastor Johnson just nodded and smiled. Keith curiously asked, "Well, what'd she say?"

"She said she knew you were a cow farmer because when you came in you smelled like cow shit," Pastor Johnson said.

Whitney was hysterical. Keith blushed; he had never heard Pastor Johnson say a curse word. Valerie blushed and smacked her grandfather on the hand. Pastor Johnson was relaxed, not the strict and Christ-minded, driven man Keith remembered from the past.

"Keith, you know, I been a preacher for fifty-five years. I always knew I wanted to be right here in Pineapple. Here at Pineapple Baptist. Just like my daddy, my granddaddy, and my great-granddaddy. The Lord has taught me a many things. And these things have strengthened my faith in the Lord. But now as I sit here, I look at you and my beautiful granddaughter and Miss Whitney and I realize I still have so much to learn. There just ain't enough time for me, for sure. My time's running out."

Valerie rolled her eyes and made a sound that said she wasn't happy with where her grandfather was taking the conversation. Keith wondered if Valerie thought her granddaddy would live forever, like Keith had once thought of his grandfather. Disgruntled, Valerie stood and cleared the empty plates off the table. Whitney helped her. Pastor Johnson gravely glanced to both women, but it was obvious he was intent on saying what he wanted to say.

"It's alright. I reckon this ain't for women to hear."

A small piece of apple crust fell from a plate on to the table and caught Pastor Johnson's eye.

"Is anybody going to finish that? Because I ain't going to let it go to waste," he said to no one and everyone.

He scooped it up and swallowed it.

"As I was saying, Keith, time's a son of a bitch. The days pass and your mind is filled with ideas, plans, and a variety of complex and even inappropriate thoughts. But there ain't enough time to act on all of them. Even today, now, I can think of twenty things that I had thought of that I was going to think more about, but damn if I didn't already forget them. It's enough to drive a man crazy. I told myself awhile back I wouldn't regret nothing. But at that time I was cocky, arrogant. I thought I could outsmart time. Now that I know time's getting closer to being expired, I can't help but have some regrets.

I ain't going to go on and tell them, because they ain't no one's business but mine. But I also realize that all them things that I thought strengthened my faith in the Lord really cast some doubt as well. I still have questions now that I'm getting closer to answer, and that scares me. What if it's true? Lord, Lord, the judgment is coming! But what's more, what if it ain't true? What if he was just another man, a mistaken man? What's next? What'll be there? Will Bessy be there? Lord, I hope so. If right now you told me I could see Bessy but had to give up my faith in the Lord, I'd choose her in a second."

Pastor Johnson paused and took a sip of his coffee. Keith had a thick lump of trepidation in his throat. He thought about Billy.

"Keith, I hope my old age rambling don't scare you. I only wanted to tell you this because I had to tell a stranger and you and Whitney is the closest thing I got to a stranger here in this small Pineapple town. People know me too well. Or, at least, they think they do. If I'd begun to say this to anyone around here, they'd look at me funny and figure it was time for me to be in the old folk home. And, let me tell you now, no old folk wants to go to an old folk home. You know, old folk have to vent out at the world, too."

Keith chuckled and looked to the wise old man. Pastor Johnson had an easy and painless smile.

"You know, Keith, you look more like old P.B. than you do look like your father," Pastor Johnson said.

P.B. was Keith's grandfather. It stood for Papa Baker, who was the father of thirteen children—six boys and seven girls. Keith's father did look like P.B., but more resembled his mother's side of the family. Some said Keith was the spitting image of P.B.

"Say, Pastor Johnson, you remember Otis Brown?" Keith asked.

"Otis Brown, the colored boy?"

"Yes, sir."

"Well, sure, I know him. Why?"

"Last night Whitney and I ate with him and his family down at their place by Gullie's River."

"Then you met Krista and the children?"

"Yes, sir."

"Lord bless them. That's a fine family. Hard working. And the little ones don't show no disrespect to their folks. What are their names again?"

"JR, Lilunk, and Ebony."

"That's right, that's right."

"Pastor, on one of the walls in their house they have an old five-string banjo hanging. I knew I was sure I'd seen it somewhere, but couldn't decide where. I asked Otis about it, but he wouldn't tell me. He told me to ask you about it."

Pastor Johnson grinned.

"You really have been gone a long time. You don't remember the stories told about that piece?"

"Pastor, I have been gone a long time, that's for sure. My memory tends to hold onto images of faces and pain, Pastor. You know, I ran hard to get out of here."

"It's funny how we run from what can heal us. Lord, Keith, I admire your courage for getting out of here in a lot of ways. I wished a lot more folk would've run out of here. You know, Pineapple ain't a bad place to be, just a hard place to be. Luckily though, Keith, you can't outrun your past. It's always following you, like a shadow—the good, the bad, and the ugly. I hope you tell your son about your past—all of it. It'll solidify your existence to him, I promise you that."

"Yes, sir. I reckon I owe him that, don't I?"

Pastor Johnson retold Keith the story of the five-string banjo:

> The market fell in '29, and of course many folks in the North lost money steadily. Though most had various sources of income, the banks weren't able to provide the money. Folks bought a lot on credit, but there wasn't enough money in circulation to support this buying and selling trend. So folks become poor.

But, for folks in the South, this depression began in the early
'20s. For us, here in Pineapple, it started well before the turn
of the century. The families in the South were farmers, only
farmers. Farming was the bread and butter, the money making.
The North would buy crops like corn, wheat, and the North
would in return provide the industrial products the South
didn't know how to manufacture. The South relied on the
North for this income and production and was directly affected
by their buying habits and trade with the North. But them
Yankees didn't rely on the South at all. If they thought the price
of a bushel of corn was too expensive, they'd go elsewhere—to
the Midwest, the West, Canada. They could even import from
Mexico or Central America. Who else could the South sell to?
Other parts of the country were producing their own crops, and
the South ain't have the resources or finances to create factories.
The South was like a groundhog stuck in a hole—nowhere to
go but deeper. And the South kept on sinking.

Now don't get me wrong. Not everybody was poor in the
South. These bigwigs that owned a lot of land—farming
land—were making money by the truckload off the work of the
small farmers—the white and colored farmers. Them bigwigs
got even richer cause they'd go around and buy up all the land so
to control it. They were triflers. They'd go to these small farmers
who owned no more than fifty acres and offer them more money
than they'd ever seen, which won't much, and even give them
a job to continue farming. The only zinger was that the profit
went to the owner, the bigwig, to distribute as he saw fit.

That's what happened to ol' P.B. in 1918. He and Mary Ann,
his wife, had thirteen young ones to look after and the times
were tough. One day the bigwig, the big ol' fat man, Lord, he
was so fat, named Bill Nelson, came to P.B. with an offer he

couldn't refuse. Ol' P.B. sold. The deal was that P.B. would sharecrop the land he once owned and give 65 percent of the profit to the owner. Folks called Bill Nelson by the name of Fat Willie. They won't being rude, that's what Bill wanted. He'd introduce himself as Fat Willie. Lord, he was a fat one. He had thick red hair, like he was an Irishman. He grew a scruffy beard, too. He always wore old, faded overalls, probably because he couldn't find a belt to fit his waist. He was from Mississippi somewhere. He had land all throughout southern Alabama and Louisiana. There were some fifteen men working for him as well. They'd go to all the sharecroppers' homes each week to collect the money that was due—the rent as he called it.

So P.B. joined some twenty-five or so other sharecropping families spread out over Wilcox County who now answered to Fat Willie. Otis's grandfather's family was one of them families as well. Now, slavery had certainly done ended, but one could hardly tell it this far south. Otis's granddaddy Unk looked after most of the colored families, who were poor and owned little land. Unk won't rich by any means, but his family was always provided for, and, well, Unk was a special human being. He had a way with people that I ain't sure how to explain.

P.B. and Unk knew each other, grew up together, but both were influenced by their time and environment. P.B. didn't care too much for colored folk, as Unk didn't care too much for white folk. They were never enemies, but they never paid much attention to each other neither.

So things were going fine for your Bakers for six months or more after being under Fat Willie. Jerry, Fat Willie's right-hand man for Wilcox County, would come to P.B.'s every Tuesday to collect the rent. And P.B. would always come through with the right amount. P.B. missed owning his own land, but the kids were in school and fed. Sometimes Fat Willie'd come with Jerry and they'd bring meat and beer for a cookout. They'd laugh and call them days Fat Tuesday. But after Fat Willie bought P.B.'s land, P.B. could tell there was a line drawn between laborer and owner. It was, of course, expected, but P.B. won't sure if he could really trust Fat Willie.

Things won't going as smoothly for Unk. He'd gotten behind with some of the money. Two of his nieces drowned down in Gullie's Pond, and this had set them back mentally and economically. Fat Willie wasn't sincere with Unk or forgiving. He threatened Unk that he'd take away his work and make him move.

One day Unk showed up at P.B.'s door to ask to borrow money to pay Fat Willie. P.B. was going to refuse, but Mary Ann talked him into it. It won't much money, but any was a lot to P.B., whose house was full.

So Unk paid back Fat Willie and Fat Willie was happy once again. Unk paid back P.B. a little each month and he'd throw in a couple of chickens, some extra sugar cane, and sometimes extra meal. But Unk's visits continued long after he'd paid back P.B. in full. They'd found a conversation piece of sorts—music. P.B. played fiddle and Unk could play about anything. They'd have picking sessions on Saturdays. Unk would bring his brothers Shawn and Tiko, who both played guitar. His wife Kiki also came and sat with Mary Ann. P.B.'s brother James played the fiddle bass, and Keith from a neighboring house would come to play the mandolin. They'd play old-timey style music and sing gospel tunes.

Unk always had his eye on P.B.'s old banjo that hung on his wall. It wasn't the nicest banjo Unk had seen, but it was by far the best sounding. And Unk had a way with it that made it

sound special. Unk often asked P.B. if he could play it. Everyone who was there knew Unk had a thing for that piece. It
became a joke to them all. Shawn said he doubted if Unk ever
got that excited playing with Kiki. James called it Baby Too.
The men all laughed, but the women never knew of their little
jokes. Kiki would've broken Unk's hand so he couldn't play it
no more, sure as the sun shines.

Then the storms started in Pineapple. In February of '20
the daughter of a colored man, who was a friend of Unk, was
showing that she was pregnant. The father was suspicious,
because the girl wasn't married and didn't have a boyfriend.
She was only fourteen. At first the girl refused to talk, but she
finally broke the jar and spilled it. The father was Jerry, Fat
Willie's right-hand man. The girl confessed she'd been raped
on numerous occasions. The girl told her mother that Jerry
said if she said a word, he'd cut her daddy's throat and then all
her brothers'.

The colored man went to Unk and told him all of what
happened to his daughter. Unk knew that he hadn't a chance
of fighting Jerry and Fat Willie about this alone. He went to
P.B. for help. Unk and P.B. had become friends during their
picking sessions, allowing the music to soften the unavoidable
racial tensions of their times. P.B. wanted to help, but didn't
want to start trouble or risk losing the little income he did
have to support his family. Unk and P.B. both knew that they
could not under any circumstances confront Fat Willie or
Jerry without the law, so they kept these meetings and their
discussions quiet, or at least tried.

Two more months passed. Unk and P.B. were quiet, as was
the girl's father. They were trying to come up with a plan so
as to show Fat Willie that Jerry was at fault. The girl began

showing more and more. Jerry didn't come by as often, but when he did he still raped that little girl. At that point she was so messed up in the head, she didn't know how to stop it. She was just a little girl.

The rapes would happen at night. Jerry always went to that house to collect the money just before sunset. After collecting he'd drive away to a small hidden pond, just a mile or two from the house and wait for Paulina. She and her sisters always went out at nighttime to fetch water, so her family suspected nothing. The girl's family was certain the raping had stopped since Paulina had confessed. She promised them she'd never let him touch her again without them knowing. She lied. Jerry had her traumatized. She was afraid he really would kill her daddy if she didn't do as she was told. She was only fourteen.

Somehow the news of these secret meetings between Unk and P.B. leaked. Perhaps James, P.B.'s brother, who was known to get drunk and start fights with the coloreds, spilled the beans. Shawn, Unk's brother, had heard from Klaudia, who worked as a cleaner at Ma's on Main Street, that James was at Ma's one night and real drunk. She said he and a group of drunk white men began telling nigger jokes and one brought up Paulina's pregnancy. One of them said, "Hey, how do you know when a nigger-ette has reached puberty? She's pregnant." Klaudia said they all laughed, then James started whispering real soft. Afterwards the men stormed out of the restaurant.

Two days later young Paulina was found dead, hanging from the old oak tree that stood by the colored's church. She was found early one morning by an old woman, Mrs. Jenkins, who was opening the church for morning prayers. The body was dripping blood from her stomach when she was found. Paulina had been stabbed four times in the stomach and then hung.

James swore up and down he had nothing to do with it. P.B. believed him, but Unk didn't, nor did most of the other blacks. Unk was even unsure if P.B. was really not in some way involved. He felt betrayed and lost most of his respect and trust in P.B.. Racial tensions in Wilcox County intensified immensely when news of this spread.

The boys who killed that little girl were never found. What's more is that it was rumored that Jerry had died as well. He had a heart attack. So now there was no use in bringing up matters with Fat Willie.

Fat Willie went to Unk and threatened him yet again. He'd heard that Unk was planning on doing something about the death of the girl, so Fat Willie started taking over 75 percent of the family's profit. He did the same with P.B. This wasn't legal, but there were no papers stating that this wasn't the original agreement, and Fat Willie could afford lawyers that could prolong this type of case for years. Fat Willie warned P.B. not to work with niggers, saying, "If you play with dirt, you bound to get dirty."

On top of all this, the Depression finally hit the South hard. Fat Willie was being suspected of tax evasion. Virtually all the companies that had once bought from him were steadily stopping their business. So what did Fat Willie decide to do? He started sending boys to burn his fields and crops to get money from insurance. He thought he was playing his cards right. He figured since the market was falling he could do better if he destroyed his own crops, claim his insurance money, then sell his land and get the hell out of Dodge.

The burnings happened all on one night—in Alabama, that is. No one was sure what exactly he did with the land he owned in Louisiana. Anyhow, the flames went up in Wilcox County on a Saturday night. Over three-fourths of the thousand acres Fat Willie owned were burned, and the smoke and fumes ruined most of the rest of the crops and land.

The fires began in the early morning on Saturday, long before folks were waking on Sunday. Some folks woke because of the dogs barking and the cows calling, but then some didn't know until the next morning. Six houses burned down along with dozens of sheds, barns, and storage rooms. Luckily no one died, but this was, it would seem now looking at it, a bit more than what Fat Willie had bargained for.

Because of how things went with the little colored girl, the colored folks got to blaming the whites and the whites got to blaming the blacks. Unk was sure it was the KKK. They were too stubborn to figure things out until Unk finally visited P.B. one day, two weeks after the fire. Unk saw how much P.B. had lost. They started putting two and two together. It didn't make sense. Who else would burn all that land? For what reason? They knew Fat Willie was behind it, but couldn't quite figure how.

They decided to go to a lawyer in Alexander, the county seat. They went to several firms telling their story, the two of them together, a rarity for the times. Most of the firms refused to defend them, seeing as though they didn't have much evidence. Fat Willie was also a well-known and rich man in Wilcox County. He was in with the all-important people of the time. He was even on the county council, which was puzzling, seeing he didn't live in the county. But he claimed since he owned over half the county that was enough for him to claim residency.

Unk and P.B. did finally find a lawyer who'd help them. Mr. Linwood Hamilton told them he'd look into it, so long as they brought him some hard evidence to work with.

Unk's brother Shawn found it. Shawn was known for his homemade sweet corn whiskey. He'd sell a half-pint for fifty cents and, by golly, that half-pint would be enough for the night. He'd sell it from his back porch, which turned into a hangout on Friday and Saturday nights. One night two white boys showed up at Shawn's with one of Shawn's Negro friends who was a regular at the joint. They had quite a bit of money they was flashing, and Shawn asked where they got it from in these low times. They ain't say nothing then, but later that night the liquor must've gotten the better of them. Them two white boys started bragging about bringing Wilcox County to its knees. One thing led to another, and the alcohol caused the beans to be spilled once again. They said they was the only three from the county in on it. Most of the other six or so boys was from Mississippi. They'd driven from Mobile that night with over two hundred gallons of petroleum and lit up the place. They burned what evidence there was and drove back to Mobile the same night. Them three boys was given one thousand dollars each to show them boys from Mississippi where to burn and to keep quiet about it.

I reckon their conscience got to them or maybe their money was running out, because they confessed to Unk and P.B. the next day as well. Unk and P.B. knew they had to keep them boys quiet, else Fat Willie would end them. They knew, too, they had to act fast. That next Monday Mr. Hamilton was visited by Unk and P.B. with news of their hard evidence. Then Linwood traveled out to P.B.'s old hunting cabin in the forests where them three boys was hiding. Linwood advised them they'd have to hide elsewhere. As soon as Fat Willie had word of this he'd for sure send his Mississippi boys searching all of southern Alabama for them three.

Linwood was satisfied with their story and had the case filed by Tuesday. The first hearing would be the following Monday.

Linwood was confident they had enough proof to convict Fat Willie. This would be the very first prosecution made by share-croppers against landowners in all of Alabama. The real true question was how would judges and jury react to such a case.

But it wouldn't matter anyhow. That Saturday two of the boys—one of the white boys and the colored boy—and Unk were shot dead. They were crossing old Route 41, which then was just a dirt road, walking through the now barren cornfields to go stay with another one of Unk's brothers, Leroy. During that week the witnesses had changed houses every day to keep hidden. I reckon they almost made it.

The boy that survived said the truck came out of nowhere. He said it was an orange truck with a large grill on the front and no plates. They were thirty yards away or more. There was one driver and two men standing in the truck bed with shotguns. They were wearing white KKK hoods. They all spotted the truck and turned to run. The boys in the truck took six shots. Unk dropped first; he was shot right square in the back—in the spine. The boy said as Unk was falling he yelled "Run." The other two didn't get much farther than Unk. Leroy found his brother and the two others dead. The surviving boy was unconscious with three gunshot wounds.

Leroy carried the boy to his house and sent for P.B. and Pineapple's doctor, who was also my daddy. He was the doctor and the preacher. Linwood came the next day. P.B., nor the surviving boy, wanted to go through with the trial. Linwood tried to convince P.B. they still had a case, but P.B. said he wouldn't do it without Unk. The other boy died a week later, so there weren't no witnesses anyway.

The charges were dropped on Fat Willie, who was nowhere to be found anyhow. A month later he was arrested for tax evasion. The land he'd owned was given over to the county and then it was rented out cheap to the sharecroppers to farm before it was resold to a new bigwig landowner.

Unk's death was a tragic loss. He was only forty-two. He was a leader, not only among the coloreds, but for all the people of Pineapple. He stood up for the sharecroppers, who were many in Wilcox County.

At the funeral service P.B. sang one of the gospel tunes they'd used to sing on his back porch together. He sang "Oh Death":

Oh, oh, oh, Death
Oh, oh, oh, Death
Won't you spare me over
'til another year?

Well, what is this, that I can't see
with ice cold hands takin' over me.
Well I am dead, none can excel,
I open the door to heaven or hell.

Oh death someone would pray
could you wait to call me another day.
The children prayed, the preacher preached,
time and mercy is out of your reach.

I'll fix your feet when you can't walk.
I'll lock your jaws till you can't talk.

I'll close your eyes so you can't see,
this very hour come and go with me.

Death I come to take the soul
I leave the body and leave it cold.
To drop the flesh off of the frame
the dirt and worm both have a claim.

Oh, oh, oh Death
Oh, oh, oh Death.
Won't you spare me over 'til another year?
Won't you spare me over 'til another year?

And that brings us to Baby Too. That old piece hung on P.B.'s wall for years and years. He didn't let anyone play it. It just sat there. Maybe it reminded him too much of ole Unk and he didn't want to see it go. That's where you seen it—hanging on your grandpa's wall. As your granddaddy got older and older he got sick as well. When he was laying on his deathbed he sent for Shawn, who was twenty years younger, and told him to take that old five-string with him. P.B. told Shawn he won't sure why he kept it hanging as long as he did, but that now it was time to let go of it. Shawn took it and hung it on his wall in his home by Gullie's River, where it has hung ever since. After Shawn died, Otis's father moved in that house and after Otis's father died Otis moved in there. I reckon Otis wanted to keep it hanging.

Keith remembered some of the story, but he'd never heard the whole of it. Keith's daddy had never told him in full, which puzzled Pastor Johnson. It was a story that many families told in Pineapple. Some folks even told it as to somehow connect their kin to it. But Keith was part of it. His blood was part of it.

Keith vaguely remembered his grandfather, but not in the way the story was told. He remembered his tobacco smoke–scented house and his grandfather's frequent forgetfulness because of his mild case of Alzheimer's disease. He remembers his father and grandfather often fighting and his grandfather's frequent use of the word "nigger." Keith's grandfather was a sharecropper, as was his father. They lived a hard life, and a part of Keith wanted to live how they did to see it so that he could feel a part of it.

He thought about the story that night lying in bed next to Whitney. Keith would never again return to Pineapple.

~ PART THREE ~

Serenity

Stuck in the Clouds

Flying thirty-five thousand feet in the air, Keith looked out the window from his seat on the plane. It was a medium-sized plane, a little over 150 passengers. They would fly from Mobile to Atlanta and then to Winston-Salem. That's as close as they'd get to Esmont by plane.

Keith enjoyed the window seat. Being that high in the sky put him in another world, both physically and mentally. It was peaceful and calm. The only distraction was the occasional turbulence and the seldom-passing flight attendant with refreshments. Keith always slept comfortably when traveling. Be it by car, train, or plane, he never had difficulty catching some shut-eye.

In the distance the clouds were large and puffy. Each unique curvature appeared full of substance—the substance pushing its way out as far as possible before plummeting from the gaseous air bubble.

Beneath the heights of the highest clouds were trees. Autumn in the South was now blooming. In Esmont many of the trees had already lost their leaves, but here, where the climate was milder, the leaves were in the midst of changing color. Yellow, orange, dark red, and light green filled the area below.

Whitney was passed out in the aisle seat next to him. Her seat was reclined. Her right arm hung to the floor while her left hand gripped a barf bag, though she was in a deep sleep.

The stewardess was approaching with beverages and peanuts. When she got to Keith and Whitney she had to place Whitney's arm in her lap so she could get through the aisle. She whispered to Keith as she handed him two small bags of salted peanuts and two small napkins.

"What would you like to drink, sir?"

"Coffee, please."

"Cream, sugar?"

"Only cream."

The stewardess wore a nametag that read "Jess." She handed Keith the coffee and creamers and then showed him a variety of newspapers.

"Reading material?"

There was the *Atlanta Journal-Constitution*, the *Birmingham News*, and the *Raleigh News and Observer*. The *AJC* front-page headline caught Keith's eye: "Mayor applauds race relations."

"No, thanks. I'll pass," Keith replied to Jess.

When they got back to Esmont it was raining as it had been doing for the four days that they were gone. It hadn't been pouring rain, but there was a constant drizzle that had left the ground soggy. Dale said he hadn't seen the sun since they'd left.

He also told Keith the cows were fine. Keith had put them in the pasture to the right of the barn. There were two watering troughs and plenty of tall pines for shade and shelter. It had plenty of thick green grass. Before he left he told Dale not to move them if it did begin to rain. Dale himself never moved when it rained anyhow, so it worked out.

"I just been sitting right here on the porch ever since it started raining."

Nellie rolled her eyes.

"Dale, you don't never move from that spot when it rains. Why? All's you do is sit and spit and sit and sip. I ain't even seen you get up to use the john, not once."

Dale just stared at Nellie. His eyes said, *Shut up, woman, you're embarrassing me*, while Nellie's retorted, *Well, honey, don't do things that's going to embarrass you, you nitwit*. They had mastered the art of marital communication without actually talking.

Keith left them silently bickering. Outside he jumped in his old beat-up truck and drove down to the barn. He spotted three groundhogs in the field to the left of the road. Keith was a good shot when firing at groundhogs. On one day he killed three with three shots at about forty-five yards from his bedroom window. Groundhogs were clever little critters and would hide as soon as they heard or saw anything. They were also a nuisance to his land. They'd dig holes everywhere, and the cows were liable to step in the holes and break a leg or skid a hoof.

He opened his window and smelled the fog. The hanging clouds were thick, and the air smelled of wet grass and trees, a damp Earth. He reached the barn and saw the cows. They were lying under the pine trees, just behind the pasture. They were all accounted for, and time seemed not to have passed since he had left.

Keith was worn out. When he returned home there was a message from Whitney. Her voice was muffled and sounded as if she'd been crying.

"Keith. Hey, it's me. When you get in, give me a call. I'd like to hear your voice. I'm okay…. Just give me a call."

Keith had only seen Whitney cry once. That was about a year ago at her grandmother's funeral. November was a particularly difficult month since her family had always spent Thanksgiving with that grandmother. She'd died two weeks before the upcoming Thanksgiving Thursday.

They'd only been seeing each other a couple of weeks when this happened. Keith went to the funeral, but only sat in the back pew and watched Whitney. It was at that funeral that Keith decided she was special to him. He saw her crying and in sorrow, but it was a true emotion, helpless and hopeless, but alive. She was so alive and full of an overflowing emotion of love that Keith never attained, nor truly understood. Keith was a thinker, a worker, a provider, but touching love was foreign to his heart and his actions. Keith loved the way Whitney loved.

Keith picked up the phone, but was hesitant to call. He was exhausted and wasn't up to talking. He needed rest. The phone rang five times. When Whitney answered, her voice sounded more calm and clearer.

"Hello."

"Whit, it's me."

"Hey."

"Everything alright?"

"Yeah. The cows all up?"

"What? Uh, yes, ma'am. Look, are you okay? You sounded upset on the phone."

"Yeah, I'm okay. I'm just a little out of it. I feel tired and then me and Michael had a fight."

"Your son Michael?"

"No, Michael's father."

"What did you have a fight about?"

"About Michael."

"Your son?"

"Yeah."

"Well, what about?"

"Michael wants him to move in with him."

"Michael wants Mike to live with him?"

"Yeah."

"Well, what did you say?"

"I said no, of course."

"And what did Mike say?"

"He said he had a right since it was—"

"No. I mean Michael, your son. What did he say?"

"Oh, well, I don't know."

"You didn't ask him?"

"No. I don't think he knows anything about it. I think Michael just brought it up."

"He did this over the phone?"

"Yeah."

"Where was Michael?"

"He's sleeping over at a friend's house."

There was a pause.

Keith was tired. He didn't agree with Whitney and she knew it.

"Michael and I agreed years ago that Mike would live with me. Years ago. Even before the divorce he always said if anything happened to us he'd want me to take Mike. Then when we did get a divorce it wasn't even an issue. Michael made arrangements for Mike to live with me. It was just understood. Now, it's been six years. Mike's only eleven. Him moving would be hard on him."

"Maybe you two should ask Mike."

Whitney began raising the tone of her voice.

"But the point is this is Michael's bringing up. Mike knows nothing about it."

"How do you know?"

"Because Mike would ask me."

"Maybe not, Whit. Maybe he was embarrassed or scared to talk with you. He is only eleven."

"You hardly know Mike. He's eleven, but we talk about everything. And he knows that I've always told him to come to me to talk about living with his daddy."

"It may be. And you're right. I don't know him very well. I'm only saying maybe you two should speak with him to see what he says."

"Keith, but I'm saying there ain't no need, because Mike didn't bring this up, Michael did."

"Yeah, well, we could keep talking in circles, but we won't get nowhere. What do you want me to say here?"

Visions of Keith's nasty divorce started coming back to him. He was tired and felt himself getting short with Whitney. He wanted to end the conversation, but wanted to say some things that would make her think about the father. Keith knew his ex-wife Jenny was too much of a mother to think of her child and her child's father.

"Keith, I didn't call you for you to support me or be my cheerleader. I don't need that. I'm a grown woman."

There was a pause, and then Whitney continued.

"Damn it, I don't know why I called you. I wanted to talk with someone, but didn't know who. Somehow I ended up calling you."

"Wait a minute, that's not what I meant. Look, Whitney, what I'm saying is I think you should talk with your son about it. Maybe it is only Michael bringing this up. But, Mike is also Michael's son. You can't let that be overlooked or ignored. I'm just speaking from experience."

There was a pause.

Whitney sighed. She was a very calm person, as was Keith. They were both almost too calm to be together. Their relationship needed a little pep, a little feistiness every once in a while to be interesting. Usually that came from people outside their relationship.

"Keith, I just don't want to lose Mike."

"Lose Mike to what? His father?"

"No. Well, maybe. I don't know."

"It's not a game. You can't lose. You can't lose at being a parent."

"I know it's not a game. But we can fail. We can. What if it's not the right decision?"

"Then you'll change it and make it as right as you can together."

"Lord, I just don't know. I'm scared."

"I was, too."

"But you're not anymore?"

"Whit, I still am, but not as much. I've learned to accept certain things about being a father ... a divorced father."

"Like what?"

"Like as much as you try you can't make your child love you how you want to be loved. You do things for your child that you think are good for him or her, but they may disagree. I've learned you have to give your child space to figure things out for himself. If not, you spend all your time living for them. Even worse, you spend your time worrying over them for nothing."

"Does Timothy love you how you want to be loved?"

"No one is loved how they want to be loved. At least as soon as someone thinks they are, they aren't."

"Hmm, now, Keith. What was that? That doesn't make sense. Besides, this is love for your child. There's a difference in love for a child and love for a lover."

"Sure, there is. But with any love—it doesn't matter whether it's for your son, your daughter, or girlfriend—I don't think a person is loved how they want to be loved. I think that's just our nature."

"Whose nature?"

"Man's nature. Our nature to be unsatisfied, to be wanting, wanting. When we think we have something perfect and special we find something to change."

"So now, Keith, you think there is no perfect love?"

"No, not really. But it's something everyone deals with differently."

"Well, Keith, I don't know. I know that about Michael, my ex-husband, but I know I love Michael, my son, and I want him to live with me. Maybe I'm being selfish or overprotective, but, damn, he's my son, and he's better off with me. His family is here. His school is here, his friends. His father is hours away. We can't ask him to change all this now. Why can't his father come here more often? He's the one that chose to leave. Why should we have to change now?"

Whitney began to sound like Jenny. Keith had more in common with Michael Senior than Whitney thought. They both chose to leave their families. He had often wondered what made men become the abandoners, but never thought he'd be one of them.

"You're right. You're completely right. But he is his son also."

"Look, Keith. I'm going to talk with Michael again. But I will not speak with Mike about this until I decide. I have custody of him, and even though Michael is his father, it is my decision for now."

There was a pause.

Whitney sighed—a sigh to end the conversation. She was tired as well. She knew Keith's divorce story, but not all the details. Keith was ashamed to admit them all.

"Keith, I know Timothy loves you and you love him. And if it's okay, I love you. I don't think about how to love you, I know I do. I hope you love me, too. But don't say yes or no, don't think, just be … with me."

"Whit, I do."

"No, not now. I know we're both tired. Let's get some sleep and we'll talk tomorrow."

They hung up after saying good-bye. They planned to meet the following night at Rosco's in town for two-step night. Whitney was a dancer. She loved dancing. Keith often just mingled when they went to Rosco's, but he sometimes danced with his riveting date.

Keith went to his bedroom window from the kitchen. He pulled the faded and tan-colored curtain to the side and looked to the fluorescent light lamppost in his backyard. He could see the rain drizzle through the glare of the beams. It fell lightly, but constantly. They were small, soft drops. Each one fell in unison as if they were following a pattern. Life seemed to fall in autumn, to Keith. The thick rain, the maple and oak leaves, the temperature, the intensity of life. It was dark. The lamp didn't exude much light, just enough to see the drops of rain.

It was nine-thirty. Keith was tired, but he felt an anxiousness that wouldn't let him go to sleep. He was thinking of their conversation and becoming increasingly frustrated. Was he a bad father? He didn't think so, but was he? Why did his son seem to choose his mother over him? Did he? What was Jenny telling Timothy about his father? Did his son even know him? Did Timothy know what he did on the farm, and even more, what kind of person he was?

Keith felt shorted. He had felt that way from the start of his and Jenny's finished relationship, but felt more obligated to let things go, so was silent. Time passed and his silence became more relaxed, more comfortable until he was afraid to break it. His expectations of fatherhood changed. His monthly checks were more consistent than the sound of his voice.

Keith picked up the phone again. He dialed his old home. He wasn't sure what he was going to say, but wanted to talk.

Little did Keith know his son was getting a blowjob from Rachel Meyerston, a sophomore in high school. Tim was a senior. It was Monday night and they were studying for a French test. Rachel wasn't actually taking French, but she was known for her unique studying techniques.

At first, the phone rang seven times. Tim and his mother didn't have an answering machine. Rachel didn't stop studying when the phone rang the first time. Tim didn't want her to, but the ringing was distracting. There was a pause and then the phone rang again. He knew it was his father. No one else ever called two times in a row. On the third ring Tim sat up. Rachel lifted her head and laid on the couch, surprised and a little sullen at Tim's decision.

"You're going to get it?"

"Yeah. I think it's my dad."

Rachel turned her head to the television across the room. A videocassette of *The Lion King* was playing. It was Tim's favorite background hook-up flick. Rachel wore gray sweatpants and a baggy T-shirt that read "MHS Soccer." Tim had on a pair of baggy shorts that read "University of Tennessee," one of the colleges to which he applied. His admission results would be in by early January. He'd always wanted to go to school in Knoxville. If he wasn't accepted, he'd attend either UNC-Chapel Hill or NC State in Raleigh. Tim wanted to go to a big school. His father wanted him to go to a small school.

"Hello."

"Tim."

"Yeah."

"It's your dad."

"Yeah. I know, Dad."

"I just called, but no one answered."

"Yeah, I was running and just caught the phone coming in."

"You were running?"

"Yeah."

"It's 9:30 at night in the middle of November."

"I just felt like running."

Rachel looked at Tim and smiled.

"Where's your mother?"

"She's at church. She should be home soon."

"Oh. She's still doing that?"

"Yeah. Her bell choir group, they're playing in a couple weeks at church, so they're practicing a couple times a week."

"You hear from Tennessee?"

"No, sir. I won't hear until January. Didn't I tell you that?"

"No. I don't think so."

"I thought I told you that. Anyways, I won't know until next year."

"How's school?"

"It's going good. We're finishing up soon for this semester, so I've been studying for exams."

"That's good."

There was a pause, and then Keith continued.

"Tim, you know I'm really proud of you. I know you work hard and I want you to know I'm here for you. If you need anything, just tell me."

"Thanks, Dad. I know. How are things with you?"

"I'm doing well, staying busy. Last week I went to Alabama."

"Alabama?"

"Yeah, it was a quick trip."

"Why did you go to Alabama?"

"Well, I was going to call you, but I figured you were busy and I didn't want to bother you."

There was a pause.

"Oh, well, that's okay. Why did you go?"

"Well, Billy, my brother—you haven't met him—but he died a couple of weeks ago and I went down there."

"Oh my gosh. Wow. You mean, my uncle, your brother, the one in and out of jail?"

"Mmm-mmm."

"How did he die?"

"Well, it's a long story, but he had been drinking a little too much and left a gas stove on and the gas killed him."

"Jesus Christ. That's crazy. When was the last time you talked to him?"

"Oh, well, I guess it's been a year or more."

"Wow, Dad. I'm sorry. Does Mom know?"

"No, I didn't call her."

"I wish you would've told me, Dad."

"Yeah, well, I knew you were busy."

There was a pause.

"Yeah. That's all right. Just call if something like that happens."

"Okay. Look, Tim, what are you doing for Thanksgiving?"

"Uh, Dad, you know, I think Andrew and Jon are coming down, and maybe Uncle Mark and Aunt Martha."

"To the house?"

"Yeah. They aren't sure yet, but they're going to call back sometime this week."

"Oh. Well, what about for Christmas? I was thinking you could come up here."

"Yeah, but, you know, Dad, I'm not sure how much time I will have off. We're going to practice a lot and we're going to have a couple of tournaments."

"Already? Usually you all don't start until January."

"Yeah, but this year we're suppose to be pretty good and the coach, uh, Coach Cline, put us in some tournaments. He wants us to practice three or four times a week during the break."

"Gosh, that's a lot. I think that's a little much. You know, Tim, you haven't spent a Christmas up here in a while. When are you going to get up here to visit?"

There was a pause.

"Dad, this year is just a little busy. I can call you back when I find out when exactly we practice. Maybe I can come up there after Christmas for a couple of days. But I'm just kind of busy with doing things this year. We have a senior dance and some other activities. And then I'm going to visit Raleigh and Chapel Hill during one week with Mom."

There was a pause.

"Well, okay, Tim. Remember, I'm up here and would like to spend some time with you."

There was a pause, and then Keith continued.

"You know, Tim, I am your father. Do you want to put sports in front of your father? This farm? There are a lot of things up here that I'd like you to be involved with. We can do things together."

"Yeah, I know, Dad. And I will. It's just I've been busy. I'll get up there soon."

"Okay, well. I'm waiting for you."

There was another pause, and then Keith continued.

"Son, keep in touch."

"Yeah, Dad, I'll call you this week and tell you about our practice schedule."

"Okay. We'll be seeing you."

"Alright, Dad. Talk to you soon."

Tim hung up the phone and jumped on Rachel.

"Fucking jerk."

They kissed and fondled each other. She stopped once to ask if everything was alright. Tim said it was, because it was. Between Keith and his son there was no "I love you" and no real genuine feeling from Tim, a trait he seemed to acquire from his distant father. It would take years of heartaches and heartbreaks for Tim to see through the frustrated feelings of his youth. At the time Tim was where he wanted to be. He didn't want to spend time on the farm and he wouldn't. But more than that, he didn't really want to spend time with his father. He didn't really know him, and they didn't share much in common as far as they both knew. They'd never spend another Christmas together.

Keith let it go once again. Was there a point in beating a dead horse? He knew his son, his own blood, didn't want to be with him. He knew he was not completely lying about his supposed basketball practices and tournaments, but he was sure he wasn't telling the full truth either. There always seemed to be an excuse and an "I'll get back to you soon."

His relationship with his son didn't seem right, it didn't feel right. Did he really love him? How would he be remembered by his son? These thoughts often floated like the clouds he'd seen from the airplane. They were just thoughts, but there was something more to them, inside them—not just cosmic gas. Growing up he'd told himself he would be the best father—a provider, a supporter, a loving father. He wanted to be those things he thought his father wasn't. *Maybe I did fail*, Keith thought. He told Whitney she couldn't fail as a parent, but he didn't have the confidence to believe that for himself. Was he a failure?

Keith walked to the cabinets above the kitchen sink. He took out a small glass and set it on the island in the middle of the room. He opened the cabinet and reached to the top for the bottle of bourbon at the back of the shelf. It was a bottle of Jack Daniels, an old bottle; it had sat for a couple of years. He seldom drank from it. He poured until the glass was half-full and walked to the door to the back deck in the room adjacent to the kitchen. Gazing out the window he couldn't see anything in front of him. To the right the glare of the fluorescent light still showed the cold, drizzling rain. He took down the bourbon with one gulp and walked back to refill the glass.

Answered Prayers

Rosco's was hardly crowded. The dreary weather had kept people in and off the beaten-up roads, even for two-step night. It started sleeting early the previous morning, a couple of hours after Keith took his last gulps of Jack Daniels for the night. The temperature was continuing to drop, and more sleet and ice were expected; no snow was predicted because it wasn't quite cold enough.

Keith and Whitney went anyway, just as they did every Tuesday night. Rosco's had a group of regulars. There were Tim and Michelle, Jean and Jude, and Paul and Marie—three married couples who were a bit older than Keith and Whitney, but bluegrass aficionados. Whitney's sister was a best friend with Jean in high school so they had a special childhood bond. The two had another common bond in that neither had ever lived anywhere other than Esmont. They grew up there, schooled there, married there, and still lived there. Jean never went to college. Whitney received her degree in early education at a small school an hour and a half out of Esmont. She had commuted every day.

It was at college that Whitney met and later married her first husband Michael. He was studying for his graduate degree in school administration. They married after they both graduated—he from graduate school, she from undergrad—in the same year. Michael took a job as a counselor at the local Esmont High School, while Whitney taught third grade at the elementary school. After being married three years they had their first and only child,

Michael Junior. Just after Michael Junior's sixth birthday Whitney and Michael divorced. Michael left to accept a principal position at a middle school in Apex, over four hours away. One of the reasons for their divorce was because of his promotion. Whitney swore she'd never let a man make her leave the Blue Ridge Valley and her family. She stuck to that. But there were many reasons. It had been rumored that Michael had cheated on her, once even trying to sleep with her cousin. Whitney swore the real reason was because she lost that certain spark for her husband. She loved him and always would—he was the father of her child—but somewhere along the line she knew he wasn't the man that would always hold her heart.

Jean, Marie, and Michelle often joked with Whitney about Keith. They'd ask things like, "So where are y'all goin' on your honeymoon?" with a straight face and serious look as if they had recently announced their marriage date. Jean was particularly playful. She'd often strut her heavyset body over to Keith and drag him on the dance floor, then whisper in his ear, laugh out loud so as to be heard, and make gestures and faces at Whitney. Keith would play along, though Whitney was always embarrassed. She always had aunts, uncles, cousins, sometimes nieces and nephews at Rosco's and didn't want them to gossip to her mother and father.

The other regulars consisted of some community elders and single men and women, mostly in their late twenties and members of the various local bands. Most bluegrass players in the area played with several bands—so there was a practice or jam session somewhere every night. A small group of high school students would also come every week and practice dancing so they'd do well with the county, district, and regional two-step and bluegrass-style dancing contests that were held every six months.

On that night Whitney's favorite group was playing, the Down the Holler Hillbillies. It wasn't their music that she liked the best, but their performance. Their fiddle player, Charlie Shed, was also a stand-up comedian and they'd always do the silliest pranks and stunts on the stage to keep everyone lively. They'd also do bluegrass renditions of hard-rock songs.

The night was slipping by fast. Whitney spent most of her time on the dance floor with some of the other ladies and men who danced longer than one song. Keith had made his rounds talking with folks about the recent weather and farming. Jean picked on her husband and Keith for discussing the same things every week.

"Ain't that much changed in a week now, gentlemen. Why don't y'all go dance? There's plenty of cute women out on the floor. Y'all don't even got to dance with your own women. We won't be mad. Heck, we don't want to dance with you toe-steppers no way."

Jude was not a dancer. He was the manager at the State Farm Insurance farming store in town and enjoyed talking with folks about business—though it usually turned out to be him doing all the talking.

During a pause in the music Whitney hurried to Keith who was sitting at a table with some other men. Paper cups flooded the red-and-white-checkered tablecloth. Keith had been watching Whitney dancing.

"You dance mighty nice, ma'am."

"Thank you, sir. I'd be mighty happy if you joined me."

"How many pair of socks did you wear tonight?"

"One, why?"

"Well, I just want to warn you ahead of time Miss Jean already told me I'm a toe-stepper, not a two-stepper."

Whitney laughed.

"I told her not to discourage you menfolk. Come on, let's dance."

"Alright."

They went to the floor and immediately Keith began stepping on Whitney's toes. They were having a good time though anyhow.

"I guess next time I will be wearin' at least two pairs of socks."

"I told you."

"Hey, I want to tell you something."

"Look, if it's about last night, I think we should try to forget."

"No, it's not that."

"Oh, what is it?"

"I'm pregnant."

Keith stopped and looked at Whitney. He stared like a deer caught in headlights.

"What?"

Whitney stopped and stepped closer to him, grabbing his hands.

"I'm pregnant."

"Are you sure?"

"Yes. I wanted to tell you last week but didn't think it a good time with your brother's funeral. Then yesterday our talk ended on a sour note, and I didn't want to do it then. I'm sorry I waited, but I was just as surprised as you and didn't know."

"Stop, stop. Don't apologize."

Keith kissed Whitney on the cheek and hugged her. Then their lips met. The song ended and the audience was clapping at the good music and dancing. Whitney shut her eyes and held her man. His silent reaction said it all to her.

"Oh my, Keith. What are we going to do?"

He whispered in her ear lightly, "We're going to raise our child."

The rest of the night they were beaming. They both looked reenergized with all the joy they held. Neither were ready for it, but together it was most certainly possible. Neither told a soul, but Jean was awfully suspicious.

"What in Lord's name is wrong with you two? Y'all both been smiling from ear to ear all night."

"Not a thing. Just the weather."

"My left foot, it's just the weather. I'm no fool now. Oh, Lord, did he finally pop the question?"

"No, ma'am."

"You lying hussy. I'll bet you he did. Give me a hug, sugar."

"No, ma'am, I swear he didn't pop the question."

"Well, whatever it is come give me a hug anyhow. Maybe some of what you got will rub off on me and I can take some home to spark old Jude. Lord knows Viagra ain't doing it."

Whitney laughed and gave Jean a hug. Keith saw this and thought she had told their secret. He didn't even consider spilling the beans to the men, especially Jude, who was still speaking about business.

They left Rosco's early. They both had early appointments to make in the morning—Whitney to a parent's meeting at school, Keith to a doc-tor's appointment in Independence. On the drive home thoughts of an unpressured fatherhood, a second chance perhaps, ran through his mind. Keith was certainly aging—now forty-seven—but felt younger and more energetic with Whitney.

When Keith got home he put his duffel bag on his bed. He still hadn't had time to unpack. At the bottom of the nylon bag he found an envelope. It was the letter addressed to him from Otis. He had completely forgot-ten it. He had intended to open it and read it before he left Alabama, but somehow it slipped his mind. This wasn't like Keith.

The envelope was faded and brown at the edges. It had been sent through the mail and left unopened for at least twenty years. He opened it at the sides—the paste on the tab had been ceiled shut. The letter was on one page. It had been written on their high school stationery. The letter read,

September 3, 1965
Dear KB,

I meant to see you before you left to go to college, but I didn't know where to find you. You weren't at home. Some folks said you were working at the Smith farm, but I knew better than to go down there.

I have to be honest with you. This summer hasn't been too much fun. For one, the crops are all but drying out and we lost money. But, more than anything I have had my mind on Dad's death. He is my hero. After he died things seemed to fall apart and I'm not sure if they've started patching together again.

Keith, I wish you the best of luck. You have been one of my closest friends. Not many folks treat us Negros with respect, but you're different. My Daddy has told me stories about our grand daddies—about how they worked together and became good friends. I hope that our friendship remains. In this divided world maybe we can set an example. We don't have to do or declare anything, we can just remain friends, which will do enough.

The authorities still haven't found out who shot Daddy—though I'm not surprised, but some of my cousins and I have found the truth. Folks in the fields said the truck was red. One of the workers from the farm has a cousin who works in Abelton County. She's a wet nurse for the white woman of the house. She told us there was a red truck at that house. According to her she saw the three men at the house before they left. She saw them loading two rifles in the truck. She also saw the owner pay each man a wad of cash. She says the driver was Chad Jenkins and the two men in the back with the rifles were Jacob Barleton, and your brother Billy.

I'm not telling you this for you to do something about this. No one will believe a woman—a black woman—anyhow. Other Negro folk have told me to stand up for my name, but I'm tired. All that pain ain't worth it.

Take care Keith. Good luck in school. I hope that I meet you again soon—hopefully somewhere out of this God for-saken state.

Your friend, Otis

Keith read the letter again, but couldn't believe his eyes. Otis's father and grandfather had both been murdered. Keith's grandfather P.B. had supported Unk, while Keith's brother had shot and killed Otis's father Kati. Keith knew Billy always found trouble, but murder? Remembering now, Keith was certain Billy worked for a Mr. Cobb in Abelton County through high school. *How could he?* Keith thought. Keith felt sick at his stomach; the mental frustrations of his past were churning. He wanted to do something, but what? He could call Otis, but say what? Could he apologize that his dead brother had shot and killed his dad over some twenty years ago? Keith wondered who did know it was Billy and if the other two men were still alive. Billy was Keith's brother, but what did that really mean now?

Grabbing a pack of matches from a kitchen drawer, Keith went to the front porch where the oil lamp sat. He lit a match and ignited the lamp. The paper quickly became ash; it was old. Burning the paper was the most feasible solution. Maybe the truth would also turn to ash, but he knew it wouldn't be that easy. Keith knew Otis didn't give him that letter to make him feel sorry for the many trials of his life. Otis wasn't that kind of person, nor was Keith the kind to accept that feeling of guilt. In fact, Keith thought Otis's point of the letter may have been to strengthen their friendship, not to burn it, as the paper easily did.

Maybe all this was just a learning experience for his aging soul. He had seen life, death, heartbreak, and love in his forty-seven years and knew he would have more to see. But what could he take from this he wasn't sure. Perhaps it'd be clear down the road, but now he was at the fork, not knowing which path to take.

The night was cool and it still rained. It stopped sleeting and throughout the day and night the temperature had risen a bit. Keith sat rocking. Briefly after the letter had burned he thought of Whitney.

The phone rang. That dreaded ring always sounded when he least wanted to talk. He put out the oil lamp and went in to catch the phone. It was Nellie.

"Keith, I didn't wake you up, did I?"

"Oh, no, ma'am."

"I heard your pickup while ago and thought you'd still be up."

Keith immediately thought there was something wrong with Dale. He was in his late seventies and his drinking and smoking habits had worsened.

"Is Dale alright?"

"Well, I guess that depends on what you mean by 'alright.' Right now he's snoring up a storm. He fell asleep on the recliner watching some space movie on the television. But, I reckon he's alright."

Nellie thought Keith's concern for the old man was charming and funny.

"Keith, Melissa had her baby early this afternoon."

Melissa, their twenty-two-year-old granddaughter, lived just across the Virginia line.

"Oh, that's great, Miss Nellie. Did she have a boy or a girl?"

"She had a girl again—named her Anna Lee—seven pounds, six ounces."

"Aw, heck."

"Yeah, I know, she wanted a boy, but we're just thankful won't no complications this time. God was taking good care of her. Anyways, Keith, we're going that way tomorrow to visit. Dale says he don't want to go, but I told him he didn't have a choice. You know how Dale gets; he just don't want to leave his land."

"Yes, ma'am, I know it."

"Well, we're supposed to have a man come by tomorrow to fix our cable. It's been out for a few weeks. Could you keep an eye out for him tomorrow and let him in?"

"Miss Nellie, I would, but tomorrow I'm headed up to Wytheville. I don't think I'll be getting back until late afternoon."

"Oh, well, that's alright. We can stop by Arnold's tomorrow on the way out. Is everything alright with you?"

"Yes, ma'am. I'm going for a checkup. Whitney has been bothering me to do so for a while now."

"Well, alright. Drive careful now, these roads aren't too good now."

"Okay, we'll do. Tell Melissa I said hello and congratulations."

"Alright, sugar."

Nellie said complications. Complications. Melissa was twenty when she had her first child. She's a strong girl, but went unconscious during labor. Whitney is thirty-four. He wondered if Whitney would have complications. Keith knew he could raise a child, but not alone. That night before going to sleep he said a prayer to God in the dark, in the quiet house, asking Him to protect the mother of his child, the woman whom he loved, and for peace of mind with the knowledge of his brother's past actions.

Soggy Bottoms and Dry Eyes

The weather began to change. It was Autumn. Leaves fell. The sun peeked through the looming clouds. By mid-afternoon the large clouds had dispersed and the sun shone. Fatigued from all the sitting and spitting and sipping and sitting, Dale rose again and took a walk. First he walked to the walnut tree just across from his drive and rusty old mailbox that had neither name nor number. Dale always walked slowly, limping on the same right leg for more than twenty years. He had gotten kicked by one of his milk cows. Stubbornly he still remembered the day as if it were yesterday. He used the story as if it was a proclamation, reason enough to explain why he'd chosen not to be a cowman like his daddy and granddaddy.

"Won't ever no cow in my seventy-some-odd years that'd let me pinch their nipples. Especially Loretta. She was the prissiest cow I ever had. Tried to kick me for all them years. Every time I'd go out to milk I'd come back sour as them Granny Smiths hanging on that apple tree in Diamond's valley. She got me good a couple times, but after the time in '70, I told myself I ain't ever going to milk another cow. I'd rather milk them billy goats than another cow. Loretta kicked me so hard in my right thigh I fell straight over and couldn't breathe right for fifteen minutes. Lawd, she got me good. That Loretta reminded me why I got into fixing cars in the first place. Papa never liked it, but I know them cows had it out for me."

Dale wore his dark-blue denim overalls, long johns, and a woolen red, black, and yellow flannel long-sleeved buttoned-down shirt. In his front two overall pockets he held two screwdrivers, a small wrench, and a package of Beech chewing tobacco.

Staring at the walnut tree Dale saw that a third of the right side had dead limbs. Keith and Dale had talked about cutting those limbs off so the rest of the tree wouldn't die. The tree was over a hundred years old. Dale's grandfather told Dale stories about how they planted it. Walnut's were scattered all around the tree's base. Dale liked to call them "nigger's toes" and joked with his great-grandchildren about eating them.

"The rest of the nigger is hanging out back," he'd say. Nellie would always give him the look of "I can't believe I married this man," while his great-grandchildren's mother would try to hush him and have to explain to the kids that their great-granddaddy was too old to know what he was saying and they weren't allowed to say the "n" word. Dale would try to defend himself saying that a Negro had told him that joke and that he, more than anyone, wasn't racist.

Dale stood leaning on the fence post, just past the walnut tree. He gazed out to Keith's pasture and then to the sun that was quickly setting.

He decided to walk, or limp, down the road aways and return by the time it was dark, knowing by then he could catch the seven o'clock news on television. Dale turned to the right to walk down the road toward Keith's barn. The weather was a brisk cool. By nightfall it would drop in the thirties. There was hardly any sound. In the air there was the quiet stillness that was a prelude to winter. Looking out onto the various surrounding hills, the area seemed motionless. Winter was soon coming, and nature was beginning to hibernate. Most of the trees were almost completely bare, due to the last week's cold, drizzling rain. The leaves that were still hanging were dark brown and withering, perhaps hours from making their final fall to the earth. Autumn had fallen, and winter was burgeoning.

Dale walked down the middle of the road. He walked slowly as usual and watched the gravel road in front of him. He never looked up, busy with his thought. Thus he missed the casual motion of nature—a group of five deer, one eight-pointer, feasting on Keith's alfalfa just below a rolling hill adjacent to the left of the road, where a pond sat. The deer didn't notice him either. The usually skittish and alert deer were as preoccupied and carefree as the cows.

He was passing a thick and tangled brush of vines, thorns, bushes, and trees to the right of the road. This brush sloped down to a small valley. In the brush he heard a loud ruffle. This caught his attention and he stopped. He thought that one of Keith's cows had somehow gotten through to his fenced area. The cows liked this area because of all the wild berries and leafed bushes. But on the other side of the brush there was a slope so steep it was a danger-ous area for them to roam. Dale approached the side of the road and peered over the fence. The brush area was too thick and dark to see any animal. He sat quietly and waited, hoping the animal would move again so he could spot where he stood. Dale was convinced it must have been a groundhog or other rodent scurrying through the brush, so he turned around to continue on his walk. Immediately he heard the ruffle and turned toward it once more. He didn't turn quickly enough—silence again. Whatever it was either was playing hide-and-seek or was just plain scared of Dale.

He peered over the slope. All of a sudden a loud pouncing came from the right of the brush, then a thunderous roar. It was a lioness roar, a roar that spoke as the king of the forest; it was a black bear. The bear ran ferociously toward the fence and Dale and stood on its two hind feet. He made another loud cry, this time showing his full mouth of sharp and bone-crushing teeth. The bear was within five feet of Dale.

Dale stood motionless. He'd always heard about what to do if one was caught in a bear's path, but all of that information had been forgotten, flushed out of his mind. In his seventy-eight years he'd never actually been this close to a bear. He'd often seen them at a close distance and even made up a few bear stories, as had most men in the area.

Dale didn't flinch, and the bear stood watching. His vicious cries became softer and softer and then he collapsed on all fours. Dale felt the earth tremble.

After a moment of sniffing the air and staring at every feature of Dale's face, the bear turned around and walked down the sloping hill, picking unripe berries and brush leaves along the way. Dale still stood flat-footed and motionless. It wasn't until after the bear descended that Dale was able to move again. When he finally came to he glanced left and right and stepped back. The earth around him was quiet and still.

He checked his body to see if he was missing anything. He noticed a soggy wetness at his buttocks. He undid one of the overalls' braces, hoping the mushiness didn't mean what he thought it meant.

"Well, I'll be God-damned. I shat myself," he said quietly to himself.

He redid the brace of his overalls and began walking back toward the walnut tree and his home. He walked a bit more hurriedly. His limp was miraculously almost gone. Why should he be ashamed, he thought. He did see a bear. He was already plotting how he would tell his story. He knew his wife would never let him forget this.

The sun was pink and dropping fast. It was almost dark when Keith was returning home. The hour-and-a-half drive from Wytheville had taken him three hours. He found himself stopping for no reason and taking wrong turns. He was not paying attention to the road or his way home. As he ascended up the road toward the walnut tree, cruising at forty-five miles per hour on the dirt road, he didn't see Dale. He almost ran him over with his old Ford F-150. Dale shouted, looking up to the darkening sky.

"Jesus, almighty, what in God's name have I done to piss you off today?"

Keith slammed on his brakes and put his truck in reverse.

"Jesus, Dale, I'm sorry, sir. I didn't see you there."

"Well, shit, it won't been a problem, but you was going so damn fast."

"I know it, sir. I apologize."

"Oh, shit, Keith, don't you worry none. I think the ol' man upstairs is trying to tell me something. I almost done lost my life twice today."

Keith put the truck in park.

"Aw, heck. What happened?"

"I saw a black bear right—there on the side of the road. He scared me half to death. I heard something down yonder and figured it was a cow, so I walked to the fence. I ain't see nothing, but after a minute or so a black bear came running at me on its two feet, roaring, and throwing its paws every which way."

"Aw, heck? A black bear?"

"Yeah, it was one of them big ones. It was a male."

"My God. What'd you do?

"Well, I did the only thing I reckoned I could do. I started picking up gravel and threw a handful at a time at the big beast. Every time I'd go to pick up I'd try to back up little by little. That bear stood there roaring and pawing at me for a good five minutes. I think I hit him good a couple of times because he finally ran on down the hill."

"Well, I'll be. You're mighty lucky, I think, Dale. I reckon these bears'll be going into hibernation soon. Are you alright?"

"Shit, that ain't the first time I had to throw stones at them bastards. He spooked me good, but I'll be alright."

Keith offered Dale a ride home, but Dale, thinking twice about his mess, refused, saying he wanted to walk back to see if he'd hear or see the bear again. He said he was going to call his son-in-law Jim to go track the bear and try to shoot him if he could. Shooting bear was illegal, unless one shot out of self-defense.

Keith left Dale on the dirt road and continued to his home. Momentarily, Keith had forgotten the thing that was on his mind, but it had begun to spread uncontrollably once more: cancer. He didn't know what was next. The following day he was to check in at the cancer patient hospital in Wytheville to undergo tests to see where the disease had spread, if indeed it had. He was reluctant to commit to going, though the doctor told him his life was certainly at stake. The doctor tried to persuade Keith to just stay at the hospital that night, but Keith refused. He said he had things to tend to. The doctor smiled, almost chuckled, and said that his cancer is what he now *had* to tend to if he wanted to have other things to tend to down the road. Keith was used to being in control of his own agenda and appointments.

Keith didn't quite understand his prognosis. He hadn't felt sick or fatigued. His body hadn't changed. He had no lumps or bumps or abnormal moles. He felt great. He was going to be a father again. Doctor Alvarez, a Mexican American, told him that his case was abnormal, but not unheard of. Cancer was as abrupt as it was silent. His type, prostate, was often even less obvious to the patient. The doctor told Keith the survival rate of prostate cancer victims was high if it was detected early.

Keith didn't know what was next. What would the next month entail? It was completely out of his control. He entered his house and headed to the kitchen. He was to leave early the next morning, and he had much to plan and to think about. Tuesday night at Rosco's seemed like weeks ago, and Alabama seemed like years passed. First, he reached for the bottle of Jack Daniels. He poured a half-glass as he usually did. Taking a deep breath he inhaled the scent of his kitchen. It still had the scent of an office. He had extended the walls of his office to make a kitchen and repair the leaking roof of four years ago. But it was his home. Whitney had often tried to freshen the room with flowers, sprays, and candles, but Keith always recognized the same scent.

Exhaling, Keith tried to relax, but he had an overwhelming feeling of disappointment. His life was suddenly no longer cyclic. It appeared to become linear, with a definite beginning and ending. He gulped down the drink and returned the bottle to the top shelf in the cabinet.

He called Whitney. He wanted to see her, but didn't want her to worry for him or about him.

"Hello."

"Whit, it's me."

"Hey, sugar."

"How are you doing?"

"I'm fine. And, you?"

"Oh, I'm alright."

"How was the doctor? Everything fine and running?"

"Yeah, well, not real sure. I'm going back tomorrow."

"Where?"

"Well, the doctor told me today that, uh, that … well, I have … I have cancer."

"Cancer?"

"Yeah … prostate cancer."

"But, how? Lord, hon. How, I mean, you don't have a lump or anything. And you're not peeing blood, right?"

"Well, the doctor says this type isn't always obvious or detectable. But it's good that it was noticed today."

"Are they sure? I mean, usually many tests are run before they conclude something like that."

"Well, Doctor Alvarez, he's uh, a Mexican American, he's about 90 or 95 percent sure it's cancer. But that's why I'm going back tomorrow. They're going to run more tests in the morning and figure out for sure."

"So are you going to stay there? Is it in Wytheville?"

"Yeah, I'll be there a couple of nights."

Whitney was silent with a rushing heart wound.

"Couldn't they have warned you earlier? I mean I've been checked every year for breast cancer. Two of my aunts had it, and ever since us girls were young, we'd been taught to be aware of things like this."

Keith would now be the one folks would refer to; he would be the cousin who had cancer or the father who had it or that farmer in Esmont with it. He wanted to be himself and not a side note.

"I'm not real sure if they could've done anything. But I'm all right. I'll be back in a couple of days."

"Keith, you have cancer. Sure, you're all right, but it *is* a serious matter."

Whitney's tone began to get serious as well. She didn't want Keith to shun his feelings as she'd seen and heard him do often.

"I know it. I will."

There was a pause.

There was a moment of silence between them. It was brief, only seconds long, and a bit awkward, but it said more to each of them than words had done. They were both scared—scared for the uncertainty that they were both entering. It was a humbling moment for both, but also a reclamation of their love for one another. They would be scared together.

Whitney now spoke softly.

"Can I come see you?"

"Oh, now? No. You might get the patient all excited and he'll have to be sedated."

"No jokes, now, sir."

"No, I ain't joking."

"Can I see you?"

"Whit, why don't you come see me tomorrow night in Wytheville? I've got a couple of things to do, then I'm going to get some rest."

Whitney was disappointed and confused.

"Alright…Can I bring you something tomorrow?"

"What?"

"It's a surprise."

"Yes, ma'am, you surely can."

"Thank you."

"Alright. Well, good night, Whit."

"Good night, Keith…Keith?"

"Yeah?"

"I love you."

"I love you, too."

They hung up. Whitney sat sobbing at her kitchen table. It was an emotional time for her for many reasons. She was letting go of held-in emotions that now streamed from her brown eyes. In her sadness for Keith—and her—there was also a happiness, though not as obvious and clear. It was a happiness felt deep in the heart, one of joy, one of excitement for the experience of being. Thoughts of birth and death were suddenly changing her perception of her life, as the falling autumn leaves turn the green grass earth to yellow, red, and brown.

Keith couldn't remember the last time he cried. He wanted to cry for Whitney and their child and his son and his life. He wanted to cry for Otis and his grandfather and for the tragedies that seemed to fall in his life. He couldn't cry. He wondered if his ego was too big to cry. If a life-threatening illness didn't make him shed tears, then what would? Keith was sincere and honest. Some relieved their emotions through their tear ducts, Keith didn't. His eyes were dry as he planned out in his mind how he would handle his farm over the next few days. When he finally laid down to sleep, he thought of his son Timothy and wondered if he should call him before leaving for Wytheville.

Unrelenting Tears and Hope in Fatherhood

Keith died on a Sunday three weeks later. A week after Doctor Alvarez told him of his prognosis he underwent chemotherapy. The cancer had spread to too many cells and body systems, but the doctor was confident that it was still treatable. He was halfway through his first chemotherapy treatment when he died during the night. Whitney had stayed with Keith every night since his chemotherapy began. The night Keith died she had gone to stay with her son Michael in Esmont. She had needed a night away from the tubes, screens, the politeness of nurses and doctors, and the cleanliness of the floors and walls. She didn't like hospitals. *How could a place be so clean on the outside, but so full of death on the inside?* she thought. She felt uncomfortable there.

For Keith, Whitney's presence was enough. They hardly spoke. What would they speak about? They spent much of their time watching television—an outside world for both of them. They tuned in to the playful quarrel on the nightly sitcoms, the sixty-minute-type shows that investigated freak stories and controversial topics, and the late-night shows that interviewed movie-star guests. They watched all day—even the silly midday game shows and soap operas. They watched other people's lives, fake persons, and forgot their own momentarily.

Every now and again Keith would ask about the farm: if it had rained, if the cattle had been picked up by Alex Cole from Galax, who'd be buying them from Keith since he was no longer able to take care of them, and if Dale had drained all the fermenting wine and bottled the finished wine for himself to drink.

Whitney found out information through Nellie. They talked every day. Whitney told Nellie about her being pregnant. Miss Nellie told Whitney she'd always considered Keith as their son.

Dale came to visit one day. It was raining on that Tuesday, but Dale visited anyway. He was still sipping and spitting.

"Well, howdy, cowboy."

"Good Lord. Ain't it raining out? What are you doing here?"

"Oh, just came to visit."

They chatted small talk for about twenty minutes, then Dale had a surprise. He reached in his inside coat pocket and pulled out a small canteen. Keith grinned at the bottle and shook his head at the seventy-eight-year old man.

"You want a swig of this here apple cider?"

"Well, I guess a swaller wouldn't hurt."

They had used those lines many times. They passed the bottle back and forth about three times before the nurse came in and caught them red-handed.

"Mr. Baker, well, my star! What is that you're drinking?"

Dale grabbed the canteen out of Keith's hand, capped it tight, and put it back in his coat pocket.

"Ma'am, that was just some spring water I brought for my—"

"I'm sorry, sir, I don't mean to be rude, but I'm asking Mr. Baker here."

"Ms. Hilma, just like this fine gentleman has told you, Mr. Dale just brought me some spring water."

The nurse gave the two a stern look and put her hands on her wide hips.

"Well, now, y'all look here. There ain't no spring water allowed in this here room or in this here hospital. Now, please tell your gentleman friend, Mr. Dale, he'd better keep his spring water in his coat or he'll be leaving this here establishment."

The two men just smiled and said, "Yes, ma'am." Dale left shortly after saying he'd caused too much trouble and that he was afraid of the "big ape-looking woman." Before he left, Keith told Dale that he wanted him to have his farm and home if anything were to happen to him. Dale told him that he was talking nonsense and that he'd be back home in no time. But Keith made him promise he'd take it, and Dale did.

Other than Dale, Tommy Cox, and a handful of Whitney's relatives, Keith didn't receive too many visitors. Timothy Simon stayed with him during one weekend. Keith told him to go to school instead to finish his exams and practice basketball. His visit was an awkward moment for them. Keith always veered away from discussing his condition, as did Tim.

Tim had felt tense entering his hospital room and finally relaxed when he left. It was difficult for him to see his father as he did, just as it was difficult for Keith to have his son see him. At one time Keith talked about his family in Alabama. He talked about his brother Billy and his mother and father and grandparents. He told Tim about how close-knit family and community were when he grew up. Then Tim asked his father why he had left. Keith was surprised at his son's question and had to think to answer. He didn't have an answer. Why did he leave his home, his community? Keith simply told Tim that after his mother and father died, he had left to continue going to school, and his interests led him to other parts, other regions.

Then Tim asked how his parents had died. He had heard a couple of stories from his mother, but had never heard from his father. Keith told him the story. His mother died when he was twenty-two and in his second year in college. She had been battling with tuberculosis for over ten years. In her last couple of years of living she was bedridden and often delirious from the medication she took. She stayed with her sister after she got too sick. Keith drove from Pensacola to attend the funeral and left the next day. Keith's father died when Keith was sixteen years old—in tenth grade. He died from all the smoking he had done, but was never diagnosed with cancer. The doctors just said his lungs were so full of smoke and tar there wasn't much room for oxygen. Keith recalled that he smoked every day until he died. Keith's granddaddy died the same way. Keith was ten. His granddaddy's house was always full of smoke. His grandfather was often sucking air from an oxygen tank. In between breaths of fresh air he'd smoke hand-rolled cigarettes.

When Tim heard of his father's death he didn't cry. Nor did he cry at the wake or funeral. Tim wasn't sure if he loved his father. It wasn't until fifteen years later that he found himself crying and sobbing for his father. He explained all this to his father in a letter that he left at his gravesite under a basket of blue and yellow wildflowers.

Dear Dad,

Brandy died today. Brandy was our Cocker-Spaniel. She was only 8 years old. The veterinarian said she had a tumor and had to be put down. The kids cried as did my wife. And, me, of course. I can't remember when I cried last. It was probably when I was 8 and I broke my collarbone swinging on the oak tree in the yard. Mom was so mad because she had told me never to play on those limbs. But, after our family had a short service for Brandy I couldn't stop crying. I didn't let the kids see me or my wife. I left home and started driving, telling everyone I was running errands. I was boohooing like a little boy.

But, it wasn't because of Brandy, though she was a damn good dog. I was crying for you, Dad. I never cried when you died or even felt exactly sad. I wasn't sure how to feel. Here you were, this man who was my father, whom I didn't really know, and then you were dead. To be honest, Dad, most of the time I was pissed at you. The one thing I thought I cared most about—sports—wasn't a big deal to you. Plus, you lived on a farm and lived this humble and hard-working life, while most of my friends' dads were out playing golf on Saturdays and driving sports cars. But, as these years have passed I guess

I've come to terms with the preconceived ideas I had about you. Now that I'm a father I feel closer to you. I know now how you felt as a father—wanting everything for your child, but not sure how to succeed in guiding them. At least, I think I know what you thought. I wish I now had you around for some advice. The kids ask about their granddaddy Baker. I tell them what I know, but what I don't I make up—I apologize for this, but I think you would approve.

You'd be awfully proud of them. Both Mark and Sarah got all A's last year, well, Sarah got a B in Science. Mark is an incredible artist. He draws all sorts of pictures. Sarah plays the piano beautifully, though she's only eight years old. Her hands are long and strong—like her grandfather's.

My wife's beautiful and a gift from God. You would approve for sure. We met back in college, back at UT.

We're going to Alabama next month. We're going to visit Pineapple. Whitney told us to visit a Mr. Otis Brown. She said he would enjoy seeing us and gave us his number and address. She also told us to ask about a banjo hanging on the wall.

Whitney is doing well. We've stayed very close over the last 10 or so years. She's a very special lady. She loved you dearly and still talks about you. Dale died last year. I didn't go to the funeral, but I heard there were many people there to support Nellie, who's now 95.

Mr. Diamond's son bought your farm a couple of years after you died. He still farms cattle and occasionally makes wine, but I hear it's not as good as yours.

I miss you, Dad. I think of you often and wonder if you're looking down on us or even right here with us. Look over my family and take care of them. I'll be in touch.

Love, Your son

A month after Keith died, Whitney had a miscarriage. She told everyone she couldn't have the child without the father. She never remarried, but still never missed dancing two-step night at Rosco's every Tuesday night.

The seasons still passed. Autumn fell year after year. The thick, green grass swayed with the brisk breeze and Crackel Mountain howled as tree branches snapped.

ACKNOWLEDGMENTS

With a humble heart and mind, I present this novel to simply share a story and hopefully inspire others to share one, as well.

Thank you, Mom and Dad, for your unending support. Thank you, Sis, for always lending an ear and offering clever and inspiring advice.

I'm forever indebted to my cousin Jeffrey and his wonderful wife Jodi, who are the most fantastic couple in the world and often the light in my heart when my imagination and creative energies are extinguished.

My dearest thanks go to Cassie Wangness, who was my first audience and encouraged me to continue writing. Thank you to Mike Emborsky, Patrick Ramsay, Tracy Bach-Lombardo, Shelby Bryant, Alan Barstow, Dave Goldwasser, Jackie Davis, Frank Berger, and Charlie Cates, who offered not only their time in reading, but their thoughtful insight to the mechanics of the art of writing (not that I have mastered it).

Thank you, Chapel Hill Press, for enabling me to publish this work and for your support and assistance with the process. I'd like to give a special thank you to Edwina Woodbury for your diligence and professionalism. It has been a pleasure working with you.

Last, but certainly not least, thank you, Jasmeen, my beautiful wife, for your continued wisdom, support, patience, and endless love.